"Sir, you can go to the fifth-floor waiting room."

Rick silently cursed fate. *Now what?* This wasn't his business. He eyed the exit door and the lift. Crazy. This was crazy, he told himself, but he shuffled into the lift because he couldn't leave Mara all alone.

When he stepped out seconds later, he saw an empty waiting room, with blue walls that were meant to soothe. Funny, he didn't feel tranquil. He paced. He checked the clock on the wall and wondered how long it took to have a baby.

Why wasn't there anyone for her to lean on? Where was the baby's father? Weary, he sank onto the window ledge. He felt drained…emotionally walloped. He'd wanted to ease her pain, to assure her everything would be all right. Jeez, it wasn't even his baby, yet he couldn't recall ever feeling so connected to someone…

Dear Reader,

We've another great selection of books for you this month, including some of your favourite authors.

Firstly, we've got a new mini-series to highlight. Trisha Alexander's *A Bride for Luke* is the first title in her THREE BRIDES AND A BABY series, which will continue early next year. Bestselling author Nora Roberts continues THE MACKADE BROTHERS series with *The Fall of Shane MacKade*—you'll love this story about the fourth brother, who certainly meets his match in Rebecca Knight!

Barbara Bretton's *Renegade Lover* is September's THAT SPECIAL WOMAN! title, whilst Jennifer Mikels' *Expecting Baby* is a tale to tug at the heartstrings! And rounding off this month is Ellen Tanner Marsh's touching *A Family of Her Own*, and Judith Yates' warm family story, *A Will and a Wedding*.

We're sure you'll be delighted with each and every one!

Sincerely,

The Editors

Expecting: Baby

JENNIFER MIKELS

All the characters in this book have no existence outside the imagination of the author, and have no relation whatsoever to anyone bearing the same name or names. They are not even distantly inspired by any individual known or unknown to the author, and all the incidents are pure invention.

All Rights Reserved including the right of reproduction in whole or in part in any form. This edition is published by arrangement with Harlequin Enterprises II B.V. The text of this publication or any part thereof may not be reproduced or transmitted in any form or by any means, electronic or mechanical, including photocopying, recording, storage in an information retrieval system, or otherwise, without the written permission of the publisher.

This book is sold subject to the condition that it shall not, by way of trade or otherwise, be lent, resold, hired out or otherwise circulated without the prior consent of the publisher in any form of binding or cover other than that in which it is published and without a similar condition including this condition being imposed on the subsequent purchaser.

Silhouette, Silhouette Special Edition and Colophon are registered trademarks of Harlequin Books S.A., used under licence.

First published in Great Britain 1996 Silhouette Books, Eton House, 18-24 Paradise Road, Richmond, Surrey TW9 1SR

© Suzanne Kuhlin 1996

ISBN 0 373 24023 6

23-9609

Printed and bound in Great Britain by Mackays of Chatham PLC, Chatham

...d leaned against the banister. The railing g...
the back stairs light fell across her. The wind flared the
bottom of her coat, blowing it open and away from
her, revealing what Rick hadn't seen before.

She was pregnant.

He decided another word should describe a woman
in the last stage before giving birth. A woman said,
"I'm pregnant," the moment the little home tester
confirmed the fact. That pregnant wasn't the same as
this, he decided, noting the swollen belly she'd now
placed a hand over.

Because he didn't want to scare her, he banged the
garbage can lid to signal someone loitered in the dark
yard.

Her head shot up, her eyes narrowing. He emerged
from the shadows, and to ease away the hint of panic
in her eyes, from feet away, he announced, "I'm the
new tenant."

Mara peered at him until he stepped into the light
from the stairway. He hadn't donned a jacket. The
wind flapped at his short-sleeve shirt and the legs of
his comfortable-looking Levi's. Like her, he appeared to have made a quick run to the garbage can,
not even bothering to tie the laces on his sneakers.
"Hi." Less anxious, she flashed an instinctive smile.
"I'm 4A. Your neighbor across the hall."

As she regrasped her garbage bag, Rick inched
closer and extended a hand toward her. Nothing

railing, she rubbed at the vague ache, hoping
would ease when she went to bed. "I was supposed to
leave the garbage bag until morning. My brother said
he'd take it down, but I couldn't stand the mess. I'm
one of those," she added when he joined her on the
steps. "The Abrams used to live in your place. It's a
nice furnished apartment, isn't it?"

The apartment suited Rick. The bay window offered him a view of the sidewalk and street in both directions.

"Are you settled in?"

"It didn't take long." He'd thought her beautiful
before. Her being pregnant hadn't changed his mind.
"I don't have much."

Mara had seen his sparse belongings earlier when
he'd unpacked his car. She'd had little choice. Her
sister Bianca, a perennial busybody, had craned her
neck to itemize what he'd unpacked.

"It's your new neighbor," Bianca had said. "Come
see."

Mara had seen enough. He had startlingly good
looks, an angular jaw, slashing cheekbones, tawny-
colored hair. A little shaggy, a little too long, it had
blown beneath the wind. Around six feet, he had a
powerful build that would have assured her he challenged his muscles daily even if she hadn't seen him
hefting a toolbox from his trunk. "Are you alone?"

Always, Rick mused. "Uh-huh."
to ask her the question. The left hand ~~i~~
mound barely concealed by her coat was ringless.

"I didn't think there was a woman. Women have trouble living with someone else's decorating. I would, anyway." She knew she was rambling, but he'd unnerved her. Hidden by the mantle of the night, he'd been so quiet. She hadn't even known anyone was near until she'd heard the crash of the garbage lid. "I like a lot of myself around me, which means any move is a big production," she added. He remained silent, and she fretted that he was annoyed because of the noise coming from her apartment earlier. "Just so you know," she said when they reached the top steps. "We don't usually make that kind of racket. But my family had a baby shower for me earlier. The baby was supposed to come in February. But it looks like she might come early." Mara hadn't been surprised when the doctor had said she'd miscalculated. So much had been happening that she'd hadn't paid attention to a missed period, and when she had, her first inclination had been to excuse it as stress.

"Definitely a she?"

"Yes. With the modern wonder called ultrasound, there's little mystery anymore about whether a woman will have a boy or a girl."

Rick reached around her to open the door. "Did you want a girl?"

Preceding him inside, Mara couldn't veil a smile. She believed only another pregnant woman would truly understand her amusement. People always asked that question, and only one answer was conceivable.

s that the baby's healthy." She am
him down the hallway and stopped at her
door. "Here I am. Thanks again." With his nod, she
briefly met his eyes, the shade of forget-me-nots, then
turned away and reached for the doorknob. She
moved into her apartment, but couldn't resist a glance
back. He'd already disappeared into the apartment
across the hall. A private man, she decided. She
doubted she would be sharing neighborly chitchats
with him as she did with other neighbors.

With a shrug, she wandered across her living room
toward the large kitchen. She spotted a slice of ricotta
cheesecake her mother had left on the counter for her.
Just what she needed, more calories.

As a rush of nausea threatened, she quickly shoved
the plate into the refrigerator. She blamed the uneasiness in her stomach on the sickly sweet icing that had
been on the cake her cousin Ginnie had brought.

Once more she rubbed at her back. It had ached for
hours, but she hadn't wanted to spoil the baby shower.
Everyone had been so wonderful. Her mother had
outdone herself, bringing dozens of Italian cookies,
the cheesecake and cannoli. Her sister Bianca had
oohed and aahed over every present. The evening had
been filled with the buzz of conversation and laughter, but she was glad to be alone.

Finally she could stretch and relax. After flicking on
the television, she eased onto the overstuffed chair and
plopped her feet onto the ottoman. She shifted three
more times, but the dull annoyance nagged at her
back, and she gave up all interest in a favorite old

movie starring Spencer Tracy and Katherine Hepburn.

Perhaps if she stood again. Scanning the gifts piled on a table, she moved closer to it and fingered the pink sleeper with lace at the collar. She held up tiny, hand-knit booties, having difficulty believing anyone could be so small. She tested the lock on the wheels of the stroller. Nothing distracted her from the discomfort.

With a hand against her back, she arched backward. Would sleep help? She went for the light switch but managed to take only one step. With a gasp, she looked down at the water rushing down her legs.

"Oh, boy. I mean, girl." Releasing a breath, Mara gaped at the puddle on the floor. A contraction followed, intense and fast. She clutched at the door frame. This wasn't supposed to happen. Little twinges first. Not powerhouse cramps.

Hugging the doorjamb, she blew out quick, short breaths. As the pain subsided, she inched her way to the sofa and rested her backside on the arm.

She called the doctor first and listened to his reassuring words: first babies don't come too quickly, she would have plenty of time. She said goodbye, even working up a smile in her voice. He'd sounded so sure. Why wasn't she convinced?

A little unsteady, she punched out her parents' phone number. To stay calm, she counted rings. After seven unanswered ones, she remembered her parents had gone to Aunt Gina's.

Her heart pounding a touch faster, she berated herself. Don't panic. She left her parents a message that she'd gone to the hospital, then started to jab out her brother's number. Forget that he wouldn't be home yet. And forget Bianca and Angelo. They were at a homeowner's meeting.

Another contraction gripped her. Too close to the last. If she called a cab or an ambulance, would either of them come in time? God, she didn't want to be alone while having her baby. If something went wrong...

Nothing would go wrong, if she left now.

She waited only until the pain passed then changed into clean underwear and slacks.

With one arm in her parka, she clung to the hallway wall and made her way to her neighbor's door. Slumped against the doorjamb, she banged on his apartment door, then worked her other arm into the jacket sleeve. *Please be home. I need you.*

The sound of the lock being unlatched filled her with relief. She barely waited for the door to open before blurting out, "I'm early."

Puzzlement etched a line between his eyebrows. "What?"

Mara gathered those words meant nothing to him. "The baby's coming. I've tried to reach my family but—" *Stop babbling.* On a shuddery breath, she struggled not to yell at him as he kept frowning and not looking the least bit receptive. "Would you drive me to the hospital?"

Now he looked stunned. "You want me...?"

Growing anxious, Mara appealed, "Please."

Solving her problem wasn't his business, and playing good-neighbor Rick didn't fall into his scheme of things. "I'll call an ambulance."

"No!" With a shoulder braced against the wall, Mara gripped his arm. "I don't think I have time to wait for one."

No time to wait. What did that mean? If she couldn't wait, would she be all right until they reached the hospital? He didn't even know where the hospital was. He wanted to refuse. Hell, how could he? Her eyes closing, she suddenly clutched his arm in a death grip. "Okay. Let me get my jacket."

An eternity seemed to pass before, almost reluctantly, she loosened her grip on him. "Please, hurry."

She said that once more when he peeled away from the curb a few minutes later.

"Which way?" Rick braked for a stop sign and peered at a street name. "I don't know the city." When she didn't respond, he shot a look at her. Her eyes appeared darker. Much darker. At the moment her face was contorting as if she were experiencing a nightmare. Time seemed vital. "Which way?" he repeated softly.

With what seemed like effort, she focused on him and presented a slim smile. "Oh, left three blocks, then right four to the traffic light, then a short left."

Silently, Rick cursed even that distance. Where the hell was the baby's father?

For a long moment Mara let the pain flow through her. "What's your name?" she asked, a little breathy.

Eric Lassiter. No, he doesn't exist anymore, Rick reminded himself. Never will again. "Rick Sloan." When she gasped, he chanced a glance away from traffic.

The pain eased from her face. "I'm Mara."

Snowflakes no longer danced in the air. They rushed at the car window. Rick fixed his eyes on traffic, on the streetlight ahead of them.

"What do you do?"

He sensed her need for conversation, anything to divert her mind from each contraction. "I'm a mechanic."

Beside him, she writhed and let out a little moan. "Are you from Chicago?"

"Texas." To distract her, he uttered a rehearsed story for anyone who asked him questions. "Work was slow, so I moved." The light ahead of them switched to red. Rick swore under his breath and braked. "Are you okay?" He swiveled another look at her. Dumb question, of course, she wasn't all right.

"We'll make it." She leaned her head back and delivered a weak smile. "Don't worry."

But he did. Sweaty hands gripped the steering wheel, and his stomach knotted. He kept wondering what he would do if she was wrong about them making it in time. He checked the street both ways, saw no approaching cars and hit the accelerator. Negotiating the car around a corner as she'd instructed, he saw the hospital. "Almost there," he assured her. He'd done a lot in his life, sneaking into offices where he didn't belong, meeting people in dark alleys. Even putting his life on the line. That had roused enough fear in him to last a lifetime. This ranked right up there with that one. His knowledge about babies amounted to zilch.

Scanning the area ahead, he zipped the car up to the curb near the door with the overhead sign indicating admittance. As he flicked off the ignition, she moaned again. Rick bounded from the car and skirted the front of it.

Though she'd opened the car door, she paused with one leg out of the car, as if the breath had been snatched from her. Her hand at her back, she blinked against snowflakes. "I might need your help out of the car."

He considered that an understatement. Unsure where to grab her, he hesitated before he slipped an arm around her broad waist to ease her off the seat.

"This is nice of you." On a deep breath, she swayed against him. "I'll—I'll be able to walk on my own in a minute."

Rick didn't think so. "Are you trying to prove there's a big *S* on your chest?"

Closing her eyes, she laughed, sort of, then protectively laid her hands on her stomach as if sheltering the baby. "For Superwoman?"

"Yeah." Snow hurling down on them, he felt her tremble. "Let's simplify this," he insisted and swept her up into his arms.

She coiled her arms around his neck and sagged against him. Softly, she murmured, not to him but to her unborn child, "You're a real live wire. Give your mama just another minute or two. Okay?"

Glistening flakes clung to her eyelashes. As she blinked against them, he drew her closer. "We'll be inside in seconds."

He thought she laughed. "The door looked so far away."

Though not ten feet from them, it suddenly seemed like miles to him, too. Rounding his shoulders, he shielded her from the cold snow rushing at them.

"This is nice of you, especially—" She sucked in a breath, pausing, the hand around his neck tightening.

Rick kicked the door open. "Especially what?" he asked when her hold eased.

"Especially since I'm no lightweight." She spoke softly, but an urgency had crept into her voice.

At the admittance desk, he eased her feet to the floor but kept his arm at her waist.

He felt the wetness of snow at the top of her head when she flattened against him as if her legs were too weak to support her.

"My name is Mara Vincetti."

"Your doctor called," the admitting nurse said, her eyes glued on the monitor, and proceeded to rattle off questions.

Dumb questions, Rick thought. What did it matter where she lived? What she needed at the moment was help.

"You're Mr. Vincetti?" the nurse questioned, finally raising her gaze from the computer screen.

The question threw him off-balance. Dumbly, Rick stared at her, then at Mara. It seemed impossible, but more color drained from her already ashen face. "I'm a friend," he answered.

Mara momentarily smiled. Her lashes fluttered for a second, and her mouth parted but no sound escaped. An eternity seemed to tick off before she opened her eyes. "Just a spasm."

He didn't believe her for a moment. The nurse mumbled something about insurance. Rick flared, disgusted by her incessant questions. "Look, you know her name, her doctor's name and her health insurance."

Beside him, Mara writhed and slumped, pressing her head into his shoulder as another wave of pain floated over her.

"Do something," Rick demanded, aiming a dark, angry look at the woman.

"It'll be only a minute more."

Rick pressed his point. "Now!" he bellowed.

Jumping from the chair, she cast an uneasy stare at him.

"Hold on," Rick said softly to Mara and brushed her bangs away from a damp forehead.

Within seconds a nurse popped out of a nearby room, pushing a wheelchair toward them.

With Mara's face buried against his throat, Rick lowered her to the now-waiting wheelchair. "A mean one, huh?"

Her fingers tight on his hand, she exhaled a long breath. "My daughter's anxious."

"You'd better accommodate her then."

Nodding, she tightened her lips together in a semblance of a smile.

Rick watched her being wheeled away. Her dark head bobbed in response to something the attendant said to her.

He had to give her credit for hanging on by her fingertips to that token smile even though her eyes had been glazed with pain.

"Sir, you can go to the fifth-floor waiting room."

Rick whipped around.

"Fifth floor," the admittance nurse repeated and pointed in the direction of the elevator, as if eager to get rid of him.

Rick silently cursed fate. *Oh, hell. Now what?* This wasn't his business. If he'd shown good sense, he wouldn't have opened his apartment door in the first place. Then he wouldn't be here now.

Indecisive, he eyed the exit door and the elevator. Crazy. This was crazy, he told himself, but he shuffled into the elevator because it played wrong to him that she'd be alone.

When the elevator doors swooshed open seconds later, a gray-haired nurse beckoned from behind a counter. "Mr. Vincetti?"

Rick saw no point in correcting her.

"It won't be long, but you can go in with her for a moment."

As she pointed at a door, Rick didn't move.

"Go on in," the woman urged, even offering an encouraging smile.

He supposed he typified some panic-stricken husband. This whole situation was dumb and out of control. He didn't want to go into that room, didn't want to get *that* involved. Then he thought again about her being alone. Someone else might not comprehend how empty that felt, but he did.

At the doorway, he halted. Against the snowy white sheet, she looked even paler, her face bathed in perspiration. Quietly he moved forward. Though he thought he hadn't made any noise, her eyes opened.

"I didn't expect to see you. But I'm glad—" Mara gave up any effort to say more. Another cramp arched her back. She panted as she'd been taught in the birthing classes. The effort barely helped, but it did give her something else to think about. She rode out the contraction, curling her fingers into the sheet.

His mind in gear again, Rick scooted a chair closer. He figured she deserved anything she wanted at the moment. If that included hand-holding, so be it. He folded his hand over hers and squeezed it. Though her skin was soft as velvet, her fingers gripped with amazing strength. He'd never been around a pregnant woman. His life, the one he used to know, had revolved around his work, around time with other men, around relationships with women who'd expected passion, not comfort or friendship.

This woman demanded more than he'd given to anyone since—more than he'd *ever* given to anyone. He took in her damp, dark hair, the perspiration-soaked hospital gown with some kind of blue design on it that clung to her slender shoulders, and he said nothing. He had no idea what to say or do.

A peacefulness settled on her face before her dark eyes locked on his. "It's nice of you to stay." She clutched his hand harder, her nails pricking his flesh. "Oh, again," she cried, and panting, she shut her eyes.

Rick looked around, saw the cloth and pan of water. Why wasn't someone helping her? He dipped the cloth in the water and wrung it. Gently, he wiped her forehead.

A weak smile barely curled the edges of her lips. "You're very kind," she managed to say.

He'd thought the same about her. She was working hard to be brave. However foolish it seemed, he wanted to help. Brushing back her damp hair, he said quietly, "If you want to yell—"

"Oh, no." A hint of laughter edged her voice. "I might scare the baby." The last word slipped out on another gasp.

"Excuse me," a voice said behind him. A nurse he hadn't seen before whisked into the room. "It's time. She said she had no one with her to go into the delivery room. We have to go now."

Concerned, Rick swung a look back at Mara.

Perspiration dotted her brow again. "I'll be fine," she said between short pants. "Thanks to you."

Thanks? He hadn't felt so damn helpless since he was nine years old. Now what should he do?

Standing in the hallway again, he watched several nurses hustling back and forth to the nurses' station. Across from it was the empty waiting room with its blue walls that were meant to soothe. He didn't feel tranquil. A woman with sparkling dark eyes and a dimpled smile had swept him into a whirlwind of emotion.

On a television, a talk-show host rambled on and laughed at his own jokes. Rick paid no attention. He paced. He checked the clock on the wall and wondered how long it took to have a baby.

She'd looked so weak, so vulnerable, so delicate. Yet she'd never cried out from the pain, not once. The most he'd heard was a soft moan. She'd been tougher than he would have expected. Maybe too tough. Why wasn't there anyone for her to lean on? She'd said she'd called her family. He didn't think there was a husband, remembering that she'd worn no ring. But even if there wasn't, where was the baby's father?

At the click of footsteps, he shot a glance over his shoulder. He'd been doing a lot of that during the past year.

Passing by, a nurse sent him a reassuring smile. This is my first, he wanted to say. And get this, I don't even know the woman.

"Guess it will be a long wait."

In response to the male voice behind him, Rick jerked around.

"We were told we're having twins." The guy appeared frazzled, his hair mussed, his jaw unshaven, his shirt buttoned crookedly. "I never expected it to be so hard."

For the women, too, Rick mused.

"I need coffee. Want some?"

Rick shook his head, then wandered to the window. A carpet of snow coated the hospital parking lot. He wanted some answers. He wanted to know if she was doing okay.

Weary, he sank onto the window ledge. He felt drained, as if he'd been strapped to a boat and shoved out onto a stormy sea. But the tiredness wasn't physical. Talk about emotional wallops. He'd experienced a real doozie. Then again, he hadn't ever given too much of himself to others, and even when he had, he couldn't recall feeling as if he'd been so connected to someone that he'd slipped beneath that person's skin.

He'd wanted to ease her pain, to take on some of it because she'd looked so fragile.

To the right of him, the elevator opened, and a woman scurried from it. "Where do we go?" she asked, her eyes filled with concern. Though gray threaded through her dark hair, she had the same delicate features, dark eyes and dimples as Mara.

Three men and another woman tagged along behind her. The woman and balding short man Rick had seen on the back stairs trailed two men, one with curly salt-and-pepper-colored hair. Rick scrutinized the youngest man. Tall and lean, he had the kind of looks women flocked toward. The husband? Boyfriend?

Reassuringly, he draped an arm around the oldest woman's shoulders. "Relax, Mama. She'll be fine."

Rick pegged the guy as the brother who was supposed to have garbage detail.

"Mara Vincetti. Where is she?" the brother demanded from the nurse behind the counter.

Beside him, Mara's mother wore an anxious expression. "What if she's had the baby?" Panic deepened the lines in her face. "She'll have been all alone."

Suddenly they were all talking at once.

"Why weren't we home?" the gray-haired man said.

"We should have stayed with her," the sister wailed.

"She's all right," the brother kept saying to calm everyone.

Tension finally oozed out of Rick. He zipped his jacket. To stay would mean answering questions. He never answered any. He pushed off the window ledge and started for the elevator, but he stalled when he reached the doors. He would like to know that she had the baby. He would like to know she was all right. It was dumb thinking. He didn't even know the woman, not really.

Punching the button on the panel by the elevator doors, he peripherally saw a man in blue hospital garb come through the double doors behind the nurses' station.

"Dr. Hunt." Mara's mother bolted to him. "Mara? Is she all right?"

In the manner of an old friend, he laid a hand on her arm. "She's just fine. And so is the baby. You have a beautiful granddaughter."

Relief slithered through Rick. Everything was A-OK. Why that mattered he didn't know, but he imagined anyone, a cop or a paramedic or a taxi driver, shared the same feelings when they'd had such an experience.

Stepping into the elevator, Rick distanced himself from the jubilant voices of her family. As the doors closed, he acknowledged he hadn't felt so good in a long time.

Chapter Two

Physical labor reaped a different kind of tiredness. After he'd worked two weeks at the garage, muscles Rick hadn't known he had were still sore.

Yawning, he plopped on the blue striped sofa that had seen better days and bent forward to unlace his work boots. He preferred sneakers. Before, he wore them almost everywhere. He was always walking somewhere to chase down a story.

He was used to sitting behind a desk and pecking at a keyboard, not challenging a stubborn lug nut or hoisting an engine. He liked the work, though. If he'd had to choose something else to do besides reporting, he'd have chosen to work with his hands.

Carl Ingram, his appointed guardian angel, would say Rick was adjusting, coming to terms with a new city and a new life. What he never said was simply assumed: Don't get too comfortable. The words weren't necessary. Rick knew he had no control of his life anymore. It was that—more than the moving or the risks or even the lack of friends—that bothered him the most. As a kid, he'd sworn he'd never let that happen to him again. Fate obviously had other plans for him, but some day he would get back on track and make a real life for himself.

He dropped the second work boot to the floor and, relaxing, slouched on his spine against a cushion. Noise from the hallway popped open his eyes. Something banged against the hallway railing. He heard footsteps on the steps, followed by more.

In one swift move he bounded off the sofa and snatched up his jacket, ready to flee to the fire escape. Dangling his jacket in his hand, he pressed his ear to the door.

"Shh, be quiet," a female reprimanded.

The voice of a younger woman carried a trace of a warning. "You'll wake the baby."

"Are you sure you'll be all right?" the first woman asked.

"I've stayed with you for two weeks, Mama. It's time for us to be home."

Though unacquainted with the first two voices, Rick recognized this one. He'd heard the same resolve in Mara's smoky voice when she'd told him not to worry during the drive to the hospital. Despite perspiration pouring off of her and her body writhing with a pain that snatched the breath from her, she'd tried to alleviate his concern. He had a feeling she was the kind who would never tell when everything wasn't okay.

"What have you got in this bag, sis?" a male voice gibed. "A ton of bricks?"

"What a wuss. I thought you were strong," she teased back.

Another feminine voice joined in to bait him lightly. "You're losing your image, brother dear."

The man muttered something unintelligible.

"Watch your mouth in front of the baby, Nick," the older woman scolded.

"Let me hold the baby while you get your key," a more raspy male voice said eagerly.

"Papa, *you* have the key."

Rick imagined Mara's expression. Dimples cutting into her cheeks, she'd made him the recipient of a patient smile when he'd displayed panic and had questioned her about directions to the hospital.

More scuffling of feet, more whispered words, then a door closed. She was home with her family in tow. She had her share of relatives. He had none. No roots. Possibly no future. Over a year ago he'd lost everything.

Not by choice, he'd become a loner.

Bracing a shoulder against the door, Rick surveyed the room before him. Silent, empty. Loneliness had haunted him before, but never quite so much as at that moment.

Mara snuggled Jessie a moment longer, then lowered her into the new bassinet. If she calculated right, she would have two hours before her daughter's next feeding. Blissfully Jessie slept, unaware of everyone's attention.

While Mara stripped off her coat, her mother readjusted the blanket on her granddaughter for the second time. "I can't get over how much hair she has."

Beaming, her husband bent forward with her. "We all have a lot of hair." Mara noticed her father had smoothed the blanket back to the way it was before his wife had fiddled with it.

"Angelo would love more," Mara's sister commented about her husband and aroused smiles from the others.

As Bianca sought the closest chair, Mara assumed they planned to stay for a while and busied herself in the kitchen, filling the coffeepot with water.

"Oh, dear, don't do that," her mother protested. "We aren't staying long."

"No, don't." Bianca surrendered any pretense that she wasn't excited and sprang to her feet to take a position over Jessie. "Instead, tell me about your neighbor," she said between coos at her niece. "Mama wouldn't let me ask you before, and since you were in her house, I didn't."

"And you shouldn't now, either," Teresa admonished.

"I don't see why not," Bianca returned with a pouty look that she'd perfected at age five.

"There isn't anything else to tell you." Mara wished she did know more about him. She scooped coffee grounds into the brewer. "He helped me." It seemed wrong that she hardly knew someone who'd been so vital during such an important moment in her life.

"I know that." Impatience seeped into her sister's voice. "But what do you know about him?" Bianca insisted.

"Yeah, what do you know?" her brother piped in.

In disbelief, Mara darted a frown from Bianca to Nick. Wasn't it enough dealing with Bianca's nosiness? Did she have to endure mutterings from a protective big brother? "Until this moment, I was happy to be home," she teasingly lamented.

Smiling, her mother consoled her with a pat on the shoulder. "It might be wise to indulge them a little."

Mara was no fool. Mama was as curious as her children.

"We do know that he's a nice man," her mother felt compelled to remind everyone.

Mara agreed. During those moments in his car and at the hospital, he'd been more than a good samaritan. He'd made her feel less alone. "I told you his name is Rick. Rick Sloan." Mara plugged in the coffee brewer. "That's all I know."

Concern darkened her father's face. "We should have been around for you. Who knows what might have happened to you knocking on a stranger's door late at night. Anything could have happened. You could have been raped or—"

Mara nearly giggled. "Papa, I was in the middle of labor. I hardly think he was interested in my body." Rejoining them in the living room, she paused beside the bassinet and fingered the lace on the blanket. "I looked like a baby elephant."

Bianca sank onto the chair again. "Are you sure that's all you know about him?"

"How would I know more? He moved in the night before I had the baby. Remember?" Mara reminded her. "You had your nose plastered to my front window, watching him."

Her sister's back straightened to a queenly posture. "I did not."

Nick snorted with what sounded like a laugh. "You always were too nosy."

Bianca sent him an affronted look. "I don't need this from you. I thought we were working together here."

"We are." His grin faded. "We want to know about this guy, Mara. Who is he?"

"Don't be puffing your chest out," Teresa scolded her son. "You should be grateful to him instead of looking to start something."

Mara let out an exasperated sigh. "Why?" she asked her mother. "Why did I have to be the baby of the family?"

Her mother's smile carried a hint of sympathy.

"Okay. Let me see." Because they all looked so eager, Mara took time strolling back to the kitchen to lounge against the counter. "What did he tell me that night?" She racked her brain to remember their conversation, then shook her head. "Nothing. He didn't tell me—wait, I do remember something."

Her father listed in her direction.

Bianca inched forward to the edge of her chair.

Nick scowled down at her with what was probably his best interrogation stare.

Even her mother stilled in anticipation.

Mara was going to disappoint them. "It's nothing earth-shattering. He's a mechanic," she said, amazed she remembered anything of their conversation that evening.

"That's a good job," her father said with an approving nod of his head.

"Yes, a good job," her mother agreed.

"Is that all?" Bianca asked, not veiling her dissatisfaction.

"Great." Nick practically snarled. "That's nothing. You don't know anything about him."

"He could be running from the authorities," Bianca murmured.

Standing near the window, Nick swung an I-don't-believe-it look at her. "You watch too much of 'America's Most Wanted.'"

Mara rushed more words in an effort to say something that might please them. "He's from Texas."

Bianca perked up again. "Does he sound like a cowboy?"

It took effort, but Mara managed not to laugh. "No, he doesn't."

Suspicion again colored her brother's voice. "Why did he split from Texas?"

"Do you ever leave your badge at home?"

"Why did he split from Texas?" he repeated.

She pitied the criminals he drilled. "Don't you have enough work, Detective Vincetti? Do you have to look for trouble?" As he opened his mouth to ask more, Mara deliberately yawned.

Predictably, her mother came to the rescue. "That's enough of all this. Can't you see she's tired?" she said more than asked, grabbing Bianca's arm and lifting her from the chair. "It's time to go."

Nick remained with legs spread and feet planted.

"You, too." Teresa nudged her son hard on the shoulder. Though her touch proved ineffectual at moving him, the wag of her finger in the direction of the door had a miraculous effect.

"I'm leaving." He sauntered toward it. "But I want to know more about him."

"Why?" Mara hooked her arm in her mother's and trailed him. "He's another tenant. Nothing more."

Bianca stalled at the doorway. "You don't plan on seeing him again?"

"Of course I'll see him again. He's my neighbor."

Impatience furrowed lines in Bianca's forehead. "You know what I mean."

Only too well did Mara know what she meant. Practically every conversation she had with her family focused on the absence of a man in her life. "How many times do I have to tell you? I'm perfectly content with my life as it is. I have Jessie now, and I have all of you," she said with an affectionate smile.

Head bent, her father zipped his jacket in preparation for the cold outside and submitted his opinion. "You need more. This time someone who's worthy of you."

"I'll second that," Nick piped in. Cupping Mara's shoulders with gloved hands, he brushed his lips across her cheek. "Be careful. I'll call."

"And I'll call." Bianca hugged her. "Don't worry," she whispered. "Someone will come along. In fact—" she pulled back abruptly, suddenly bright eyed, as if a new thought had clicked in her head "—Angelo has a new employee at the shop. An experienced butcher and—"

Mara jumped in. "Forget it."

"I've seen him," her father whispered in her ear. "You wouldn't like him. No neck."

Mara returned his squeezing hug and gave him a quick kiss on the cheek. "Bye, Papa."

"Bye, my little one."

Always the last one out the door, her mother patted her cheek affectionately. "They love you."

Mara felt a smile tugging at the edges of her lips. "I know. And I love them."

She received a final hug and departing words of wisdom from her mother. "There's someone special for you. We know that."

Despite her mother's casual tone, a trace of maternal concern had come through. On a long breath, Mara shut the door. Why did every visit with them always end with the same conversation? *We've got to find a man for Mara.*

She hadn't lied when she'd told them she was content. She had everything she wanted in life. She didn't need someone else.

Her family disagreed.

Of course, they would. Her parents had been happily married for thirty-nine years. Her sister Bianca was still so in love with her husband Angelo after ten years that she beamed whenever he came in the room.

All of them had experienced connubial bliss, except for Nick. But then, satisfied with his job and an active social life, he might never take the marital plunge.

She, though, had lived through the downside of marriage. Some men ranked as jerks. Some, not all, she reminded herself. One, a stranger, had revealed kindness and a caring nature.

Though she'd previously shunned her family's matchmaking efforts, Vincetti optimism was too ingrained for her to rule out the idea of marriage, especially one as lasting and wonderful as her parents had.

There had been times when she'd been pregnant when, feeling blue, she'd yearned for someone's strong arms around her, for a warm body beside her in bed.

A nice fantasy, she reflected. Fanciful thoughts belonged to someone else, not her. From the time she was eight, when she'd peddled homemade lemonade on the street, she'd been practical. Despite the family hovering so near all the time, she believed in taking care of herself. When life had thrown a curve at her, she'd bounced back with amazing resiliency. She'd had little choice. Pregnant then, she'd had someone else to think about. The gift of her child had kept her going. Two weeks ago she'd learned about miracles, about a happiness she'd never imagined. All that mattered now was Jessie.

Running a hand gently over her daughter's dark hair, Mara swelled with joy. The first time the nurse had placed Jessie in her arms, she'd cried. Tears of joy, she'd told her family, having seen their worried frowns. She'd understood their anxiousness. Just as they'd shared her happiness when Jessie was born, they'd tried to shoulder her anguish through a difficult time months ago. But all of what she'd endured was behind her now.

Leaning over, Mara kissed her daughter's forehead. She slept peacefully, her hand curled around the pink satin edge of her blanket, her bowed mouth slightly parted. She was so beautiful, so trusting. *Be careful, darling. Not everyone can be trusted. Some people tell lies that can shatter you.*

With care, Mara transferred the bassinet from the living room to the bedroom, then grabbed a moment to relax with a cup of coffee. She had plans for her future. And she had her baby. It was time for a new beginning.

But something remained unresolved. She owed her neighbor more than gratitude. Without him, she might have had her baby on the landing of the apartment building.

She smiled as an image flashed back. Despite Rick Sloan's macho image, he'd stared with masculine panic at her when she'd stood at his door and announced she was having her baby. His wary blue eyes had clouded with confusion. The grooves that bracketed his mouth, smile lines, had deepened. *Smile lines.* At one time, he must have done a lot of smiling.

He probably knocked the breath from a woman when he turned the full force of his smile on her. Mara couldn't say. She'd never seen him smile, but men with athletic builds and long legs and smiles that rocked women tended to be downright dangerous.

Pregnancy hadn't made her blind or immune to his good looks. That was something she wouldn't have admitted to her family. Romantics, all of them. They were convinced there was a perfect man for her.

Bored, Rick abandoned any hope of getting interested in the sitcom blaring from his television set. Because of the new job, he'd been too tired to explore the neighborhood yet. Tomorrow he would locate the closest library or bookstore.

He peered at his watch. Seven o'clock. Too early for bed unless someone was beside him. Not smart thinking, he reminded himself. A woman would only complicate his life.

He ambled to the television and flicked it off, then dropped back to the sofa. Closing his eyes, he considered going to a movie. It was time to mingle with people, but he would avoid getting too close to anyone. Familiarity meant questions. He couldn't afford anything but casual relationships.

At a soft rap on the door, his eyes snapped open. No one had his address, not even his co-workers. Instinctively, he snatched up his boots and wiggled his feet into them. The possibility of running down Chicago streets in his socks on a cold winter night bordered on idiocy. "Who is it?" he called out.

"Mara."

Fool. He was a damn fool. He slipped the chain off the door, wondering if he would ever completely rid himself of the edginess he'd developed during the past year.

Opening the door, he was hit instantly by an obvious fact. She looked wonderful. He'd had no idea what her figure looked like before pregnancy, but she'd had all the rest of the right trimmings. Delicate looking, with a flawless complexion and an enticing, full bottom lip, she had dark eyes that a man could lose himself in.

She was the kind of woman a man would notice, might even have a hard time not thinking about. It was difficult for him to believe she'd recently had a baby. Her shiny dark hair was fluffier around her face. He caught a whiff of the same fragrance that had drifted to him when he'd carried her into the hospital.

Full of warmth and friendliness, her dark eyes smiled at him. "I came to thank you formally. Will you come over for some cannoli?"

He wanted to say yes, he discovered. But for all he knew, a husband, momentarily in the dog house, might reappear. "That's not necessary."

"I know it's not." She flashed another winning smile at him. "Please, at least, let me do this."

Rick curled his fingers around the doorknob. "You don't owe me anything."

Laughter colored her voice. "Oh, yes, I do. A great deal. Come on. It's good cannoli. Homemade. You do like cannoli, don't you?" Mara rambled on, sensing he planned to refuse. "And since I'm not hesitant to brag, I'll tell you that I also make a great cup of coffee."

Rick doubted there was much she didn't do well. While uneasy over her invitation, he considered his options. If he bluntly said no, would he arouse her suspicions?

"Please. Let me repay you somehow," Mara appealed. She hadn't expected so much opposition. All she was offering was coffee and dessert. Though she'd already guessed he was a loner by choice, his reluctance bothered her. She'd been raised in a gregarious family that tended to reach out to others rather than turn away.

Rick saw a flicker of inquisitiveness in her eyes and quickly gauged the situation. He knew that when he'd met resistance while covering a story for the newspaper, he'd been more determined to learn what the person was hiding. It made sense that spending a few minutes with her might stir fewer questions about him. Rick seized his keys from a table by the door. "Okay."

"Good. Coffee's already made." Mara whirled away, anxious about leaving Jessie alone even for a minute.

Rick followed and shut her door behind him. Because observing had been such a part of his life before, he never entered a room now without analyzing. A step into her apartment, he knew nothing about her friendliness was phony.

Her apartment oozed warmth and had an abundance of Early American furniture. It wasn't *Better Homes and Gardens* perfect. She had eclectic taste. In a corner of the room, she'd nestled two Oriental vases together and had filled them with dried flowers. A sombrero adorned the wall above them. To the left of it hung a print of an Andrew Wyeth painting, and in a far corner of the kitchen was a one-foot-high Snoopy cookie jar.

Mara peered inside the refrigerator. "I wasn't sure that my brother bought milk. He came over earlier today and restocked my refrigerator." She directed a smile over her shoulder at him. "So sugar or milk or—"

"Black," Rick answered while taking a lengthy look at her. She was more angles than curves. Snug, washed-out jeans emphasized slim hips and long legs. She turned slightly, revealing a nearly flat midsection. "You weren't in the hospital all this time, were you?" While she poured coffee, he cast an uneasy look down the apartment hallway. Sometimes he felt like a kid afraid of the bogeyman.

"No, I wasn't," Mara answered. Motioning with her head to one of the chairs at the kitchen table, she set down a cup. "The hospital whisks new mothers and their babies out within a day. Sometimes two."

As she returned to the counter, Rick watched small, slender hands moving the cannoli to a plate. A long time had passed since he'd enjoyed the sight of a woman puttering around a kitchen. The experience was more pleasant than he remembered.

"I was staying with my parents. They insisted." With his attention on her, pleasant tension slithered through her. She accepted it as natural because it had been months since she'd been alone with any man who wasn't a relative. She set the plate and a fork before him. "It was time to go home," she said as nerves settled. "Or I'd have been so pampered that I wouldn't know how to stand being alone."

Rick could have told her that a person got used to not hearing another's voice. He'd learned to be content with only his own thoughts during most of his waking hours. But he was cognizant of how much he'd missed one-on-one conversation and the nearness of a woman's softness. When she sat across from him, minus a plate for herself, he stilled his fork in midair. "Aren't you having any?"

"I'm not eating for two anymore. If I don't skip the sweets, I'll never lose weight."

Not her words but her husky laugh nearly made him smile.

With his silence, Mara decided she would have to carry the conversation for a while. Eventually he'd relax with her; most people did. "Have you met the other tenants?"

Rick had purposely avoided them. "Not yet," he mumbled between bites and dug his fork into more of the thick cream oozing out of the rolled pastry.

"Oh, you'll like them," Mara breezed on. "They're all so nice. If I thought I could have gotten down the stairs, I wouldn't have bothered you that night. Mr. Torrence is always home."

"No problem." That wasn't entirely true. He stretched his legs out under the table. Too much close contact with anyone could spell trouble for him or the other person.

"You're still being so nice." A little nervously, she brushed at strands of her hair. "Are you beginning to feel more at home?"

It occurred to him that he hadn't had this long of a conversation with anyone except Carl Ingram during the past four months. "It takes time." Actually, no place was home anymore.

Mara sipped her coffee. "I bet all that moving around has been hard on your family."

"No family. Except a cousin I don't see often," he added, because that was the story Carl had devised for his own existence in Rick's life should he ever need to be explained.

Mara spoke her thought. "I can't imagine not having family."

"You don't miss what you've never had." Again, he'd told the truth. By her frown, he sensed she would think differently. "Do you have a big family?"

"Not too big, but noisy. My brother and sister consider arguing a token of love. Bianca's husband, Angelo, is a butcher, and my parents own the restaurant a few blocks down the street. The one on the corner," she said, hoping if she opened up with him, then he would reciprocate. "Ten, no eleven years ago, Angelo made a business deal with my father to provide meat at a good cost. When he came in, my sister Bianca swooned."

Rick raised his gaze from his plate. She had incredible eyes, he thought not for the first time.

"Angelo is swarthy, short and balding, and simply wonderful to Bianca." She propped her elbows on the table and rested her chin in her hands. "And my brother, the one who you'll see hanging around here more than necessary and who possesses the dark glinty glare and the smile that tends to buckle women's knees, is a cop."

And suspicious, Rick assumed while finishing the last of the dessert. "It was good." He pushed back his chair and stood. A woman on her own with a baby had enough to deal with. The less contact he had with her, the better she would be.

Strange man, Mara decided. If he didn't want a friend, she couldn't do anything more. She nudged back her chair to walk him to the door but he wasn't moving.

Rick stepped closer to a lithograph of Venice on the wall. One summer vacation during college, he'd been to the exact spot. Those were carefree days when he hadn't a serious thought in his mind.

"I love that." Ever since she'd received the artwork, Mara had been impressed with the serenity in it. "My parents went to Venice and brought it back for me."

As her voice floated over him, so did a realization. He'd turned his back on her. Strange how something so insignificant to someone else could mean so much to him. Decades, instead of a year, had seemed to pass since he'd trusted anyone enough to chance getting blindsided. "I'd better go."

Mara nodded, feeling as if she'd been on a treadmill. He'd been polite and pleasant—and guarded. He'd also been too kind for her to ignore how lonely he must be in a new city. "Don't you want to see her?" she asked before he took another step away.

Rick knew she meant the baby. He'd never been crazy about kids. In fairness to himself, he'd never considered what it would mean to have one. There hadn't been any woman that special in his life.

"Sure," he agreed for her sake, sensing she would be confused or, as a new mother, insulted if he refused.

Shoving a hand in his pocket, he followed her to a dark bedroom. The first thing he noticed was that her scent lingered in the air. A dim light on a dresser revealed an image of a bed lavished with an overabundance of throw pillows. In a corner of the room was what looked to him like a white frilly basket on legs. He forgot what they called those things.

"She's sleeping," Mara said, breaking into his thoughts.

Rick looked down. The baby wasn't bald. He'd expected her to be because he'd heard most babies were. Proud fathers with cigars in hand used to pass them around at the newspaper while describing in glowing terms everything about their new offspring, from the kid's bald head to its tiny feet.

Mara's daughter had a thick thatch of hair that was the color of her mother's. A subtle sweet smell clung to the air around her. Nothing had ever smelled so pleasantly sweet to him before.

She was much smaller that he'd expected, and though her body was chubby, her features were as delicate as Mara's. He wanted to touch her but didn't. She looked too fragile. In amusement, he watched her eyebrows vee slightly. Her mouth puckered as if anticipating food. For the moment, her fist satisfied.

"I named her Jessica," Mara said. "It took effort, but I found a name that didn't belong to another Vincetti," she added softly.

"Jessica Vincetti's a nice name." Rick rarely asked others questions that were too personal. To do so meant leaving himself open to be asked some. This was different. He'd watched over her on a night when some other man should have been at her side. "What about her father? Does he like it?" he asked low to keep from waking the baby.

Though her stare didn't waver from her daughter, Rick noted the deepening line of a frown between her eyebrows. "He doesn't know she's been born. I gave her my family's last name."

Inclining his head, Rick tried to see her eyes, but as she looked down, her hair framed her face. "You didn't tell him?"

In a prideful move, she raised her chin. "He wouldn't want to know." She led the way out of the bedroom to the front door. "My husband left when I was two months pregnant."

Rick wished he'd never asked. At her apartment door, he stilled. He wasn't sure why he stopped, but turning around, he found her only inches from him.

Mara let her gaze drift to his eyes—eyes that made her feel caressed even when he wasn't touching her.

Though he acknowledged the danger in his own actions, he skimmed a fingertip down her cheek. "Your daughter—she's beautiful."

At some moment, one of them had stepped closer. With only inches separating them, the heat of his breath fluttered across her cheek. "Thank you." Sensation spiked through her. This time she could name it—excitement.

"Like you," he said so softly the words whispered on the air.

And then he smiled at her.

It softened his features, warmed the coldness in his eyes. It quickened her heart.

"Night, Mara."

She drew in a deep breath. Though unsure, she thought she'd responded. He'd been so close, and she'd seen need in his eyes. More disturbing, she'd felt it within herself.

Closing the door, she let out a long calming breath. She couldn't ignore the pressure in her chest. With a smile, he'd challenged every feminine instinct within her. Dangerous. He was definitely too dangerous—especially for a woman who'd learned the hard way that she trusted too easily.

Chapter Three

Rick went to sleep thinking about her. And he awoke thinking about her. He wasn't stupid to his own feelings. Experience assured him he was attracted to her. To those dark eyes that sparkled when she talked, to that husky laugh that made a man wish he was touching her. She wasn't like other women he'd known. They lived as fast-paced an existence as he used to. Career women who matched his ambition, who wanted nothing more from him than he was willing to give.

Mara was different. She seemed comfortable and pleased with her life in that quiet apartment of hers, surrounded by her homey possessions. And she was a mother. Her world revolved around a baby, not around getting the best modeling assignment or proving herself in a courtroom or discovering why some microorganism existed. Yet she seemed as confident, as satisfied as any of those women. And a lot more content despite what Rick guessed were some weighty problems in her life.

So in her own unique way, she was his type. And damn, he had no business even thinking that way about her. Because unlike the women in his past, she was rooted in commitment to family, and he couldn't even be sure where he would be or what he would be doing tomorrow.

With a glance at the clock on the dresser, Rick rolled out of bed. A gray dawn filtered light into the rooms, and he wondered if he would ever get accustomed to six-in-the-morning wake-ups. When he'd worked for the newspaper, he used to stroll in to the newsroom after nine, aware his day might not end until that time in the evening.

Today he would have an engine overhauled by nine in the morning.

Not bothering to hit the light switch, he padded to the bathroom for a hot shower.

Twenty minutes later he locked his apartment door and headed for the stairs. A light shone under Mara's door. He doubted she was an early riser by choice. Though he knew little about babies, he'd heard they tended to mix up day and night.

Yawning, Mara shifted in a corner of the sofa, tucking her legs beneath her, and adjusted Jessie in her arms. As her daughter hungrily took her breakfast from the bottle, Mara tilted her head toward the sound of footsteps in the hall. Since waking, she'd spent entirely too much time thinking about Rick, all because he'd complimented her last night. That had surprised her. He didn't seem prone to spieling out quiet praises to a woman.

He wasn't really even her type. Too moody, too reclusive. She liked outgoing men. Her ex-husband had been Mr. Personality. As a salesman, Steve had perfected the skill of charming anyone. From the moment she'd met him, she'd been enchanted. That might have been her first mistake. If she'd viewed him more objectively, she might have seen what a phony he was.

Secrets. Steve had had plenty. She knew now the danger, the heartbreak that a man with secrets could give a woman.

Friday mornings at Bowman's Garage started hectically with car owners eager for repairs before the weekend.

Several feet from Rick, Wes Genner's mouth was moving, but Rick couldn't decipher any of his coworker's words over the noise of an impact wrench being used by another mechanic inside one of the mechanics' stalls.

"I said that I know a great lady," Wes yelled.

Rick gave him a crooked grin and resumed his search for a broken hose under the raised hood of a station wagon.

As the other mechanic shut off the tool, a sudden quietness ensued, and Wes's voice boomed. "You're not paying attention." Around the same age as Rick,

Wes enjoyed an active social life. Rick liked Wes because he tended to be straightforward, almost blunt, which Rick liked, too, because so much of his own life skirted the truth.

"I know you haven't met anyone yet." Wes lounged against the fender of the wagon. "You haven't been in town long enough. Now, I can fix you up with Rhonda. She's cute, curvy and eager for a good time."

Rick considered his suggestion. Wasn't that all he was looking for right now? A good time.

"We could double," Wes added as an incentive, then grinned.

Rick found the conversation amusing. He'd had a decent social life before. Never had he needed someone hand-holding him through a date with a new woman. "What's with you? Are you on a mission?"

"You haven't met anyone yet, have you?"

Sure he had. He'd met a slender brunette with flashing dark eyes. A woman with a smile that lit up her whole face. A woman with a smoky voice that made him want to be silent just to hear it. A woman with a baby. "Okay," he agreed to get Wes off his back. One date couldn't hurt. In fact, Rick thought it might help him. Thoughts of Mara had intruded too much already this morning.

Wes gave him a hearty slap on the back. "Great. I'll set it up and let you know what time tonight."

With time to spare before the date, on the way home from work Rick stopped at the library two blocks from his apartment building. He yearned for the books he'd collected through the years, including a rare first edition of *The Maltese Falcon,* which had been on the bookshelf in his Miami apartment beside an autographed copy of Leon Uris's *Exodus.*

Along with the books, he'd left photographs of friends, his father's watch, a baseball signed by Mickey Mantle and a life he'd been content and happy with.

While working at the Miami newspaper, he'd never seen himself as a crusading reporter. He'd simply enjoyed digging for facts, but he'd dug too deeply for one story. And everything had spun out of control after his investigation revealed that Frank Van, a pillar of Miami society whose name had been mentioned for a political office, was linked not only to a small-time hood who was dealing drugs but also to a crime network.

On the day Van had been arrested, Rick had felt smug in the knowledge that he'd nailed him, that one less kid might get strung out on drugs because of the evidence he'd gathered against Van. He still felt that way.

But a little self-pity crept in whenever he let his guard down. At unexpected moments, he missed old friends, the chase for a story.

He reminded himself that it took time to adjust to a new life. Already he'd made a few friends at work. More than anything, he wanted normalcy in his life. That was like a pipe dream. How could anything ever be normal if he had to live his life never connecting with anyone? Yet he had no choice. He couldn't get too friendly with other people. His survival depended on noninvolvement.

Right after Rick opened the front door of the apartment building, the manager's wife, all five feet one and 140 pounds of her, trapped him on the staircase.

"Everyone likes chocolate-chip cookies," Mrs. Torrence insisted, holding out a plate of cookies. "Whenever I make them, my grandchildren gobble them up. But I saved some for you. Since you're new to Chicago, and you don't have any relatives here. Do you?"

Rick shook his head and answered as expected. "This is nice of you. Thanks."

"Oh, you're welcome." Mrs. Torrence's plump face widened with a smile before she disappeared into her apartment.

For a long moment Rick stared at the cookies on the plate. They looked delicious, but he wouldn't eat one. Though the idea of a seventy-plus woman working for Van sounded ludicrous, he'd learned to live too cautiously to take any chances.

He climbed the steps to his apartment, hoping for the day when he'd stop jumping at the sight of his own shadow.

The lock on his apartment door clicked in unison with the sound of a baby's wail. Rick couldn't help smiling. It was a gusty, healthy cry that he assumed signaled hunger. Sometimes it paid to take chances. He was glad now that he had on the night Mara had appeared at his door, wincing with labor pains. In a peculiar way, he felt linked to her and her baby. He doubted any man could go through that experience and not feel something for the woman and child. And in a private way, he didn't feel so alone anymore.

As he always did, he secured the lock before stripping off his jacket. The arranged date tonight meant he didn't have to think about making dinner. That alone made this evening better than most since cooking ranked at the bottom of his list of abilities. Heading toward the bathroom to shower, he was a step from the door when the phone rang.

Rick swung around and grabbed the receiver, certain who was calling.

Carl Ingram's familiar voice answered his hello with no greeting. "You're late coming home. I called twice earlier."

Sinking to a chair, Rick cradled the receiver between his jaw and shoulder and bent over to untie his boots. "We've been busy at the garage."

Carl, a chief deputy with the Witness Security Program, had become Rick's guardian angel. He'd provided Eric Lassiter with a new birth certificate, Social Security card, even a phony résumé. But no history. How could there be? The investigation, the endless trial, the weeks at a safe house, and then relocation had swept away his past.

For a year, Dallas had been a safe haven. Then word had leaked to the U.S. Marshal. Van's men had found Eric Lassiter. Only in Texas, his name had been Eric Lambert.

Another middle-of-the-night departure, a move to Chicago, a name change, and Rick Sloan had been born. Everything had been fabricated for the second time. Carl had suggested work totally removed from writing to prevent Van from tracing Rick. Fortunately, Rick had spent years of his youth working in a car-repair shop. A mechanic seemed like a natural substitute choice for an occupation.

"Did you hear me?" Carl asked, indicating he'd repeated himself. "We finally finished a background check on all the tenants. They've all lived there three years or more. Some of them, like the Torrences and Weisman, have been there for twenty. So you can relax. You're safe in your apartment building."

Rick eyed Mrs. Torrence's chocolate-chip cookies, then reached forward for one.

"What about the writing? Are you writing?"

How could he not? Writing was in his blood. Carl understood that need, had even suggested Rick try his hand at fiction. "In my spare time. I'm almost finished with the manuscript."

"You're handling the move better this time."

Rick understood the deeper meaning in Carl's comment. In Texas, he hadn't hidden his resentment at all. "Resignation has finally settled in."

"Is that the truth?"

"Would I lie?" Rick asked and laughed at the irony of his own comment. Lies flowed from his mouth to everyone since he'd become a part of the Witness Security Program. Dutifully, he filled Carl in on the so-called excitement in his life. "I joined a fitness center. And I've got a date tonight. Do I sound normal?"

"I always thought you were."

But was he? he wondered, after finishing the call.

Rick shuffled into the bathroom. It seemed ironic to him that Van sat in a cell in prison, but not only he had lost his freedom.

Twenty minutes later, shaved, showered and dressed, he found that his enthusiasm about the date had waned. With effort, he slid into his jacket.

Opening the door, he froze. On the landing, a freckle-faced kid in a delivery man's uniform shifted a package and tucked it under his arm before reaching inside his jacket. "I've got a package for Mara Vincetti."

Despite Carl's reassuring words about his safety, Rick riveted his eyes on the guy's hand. The delivery man's uniform looked legitimate, but Rick didn't relax until the kid had retrieved a pen. "She's in the other apartment."

The kid impatiently tapped his pen on the clipboard. "No one answers. Would you sign for it?"

Icy streets and knee-high drifts of snow had tangled traffic and kept anyone with sense homebound. So why hadn't she answered her door? Rick nodded and took the pen from the delivery boy. He almost made a royal mistake and signed Eric Lassiter.

Taking back his clipboard, the kid thrust the package at Rick. It jingled. "Sounds like a toy, don't it?"

Rick merely nodded. He seesawed mentally over what to do with the package. The smart thing would be to leave it outside Mara's door.

Mara wrapped a towel around her wet hair and quickly slipped on jeans and an oversize sweatshirt. The warm water had helped ease muscles rebelling at the self-imposed punishment of a daily exercise program.

Barefoot, she padded into the living room to check on Jessie in her playpen. Her daughter's eyes widened at the turban, stirring Mara's laugh. She unwound the towel, letting her hair tumble around her face. "It's Mommy," she assured her daughter and received a reward of a smile. "Oh, you're so—" She cut her words short at the rap on her door. She expected no one, but then her family tended to come unannounced whenever the mood hit them. Quickly towel-drying her hair, she did as her father had insisted since she'd been living alone. "Who is it?" she asked.

"Rick."

Perfect timing for a visit. She fingered her wet hair. She was vain enough to hate the idea of opening her door with her hair dripping.

She squatted before the television screen to use it as a mirror and, making a face at herself, fluffed her hair.

The moment she opened the door, Rick caught the scent of soap and a clean spring day. An aqua sweat-shirt and snug jeans emphasized how slender she was. Her skin glowed from the moisture beading it. Damp strands curtained her face. It took effort to resist touching one errant curl curving toward her cheek. As her eyes shifted to the box in his hands, he remembered why he'd knocked. "This came for you."

"I didn't order anything," she said about the package in his hand.

"It jingles."

"Oh." Mara scanned the return address. "I bet it's a gift for Jessie from my Uncle Louie." Like a child eagerly opening a Christmas present, she tore at the brown paper covering the box and backed up. "Come in."

Damn, he wanted to. Rick hadn't realized how much he wanted to until he'd stood facing Mara. Carl's words came back to him. *We checked out the tenants. You're safe in your apartment building.* He smelled the rich aroma of coffee and eyed the pot longingly. What he yearned for more, though, was companionship.

Balling the brown paper, Mara caught the direction of his stare. "Want some?" she asked, tossing the paper into her garbage receptacle. He smiled. No stingy one this time. It was like the one last night, full and devastating.

"I could use a cup. All I've got at my place is left over from last night."

Mara finished opening the package and removed a bright yellow roly-poly toy with a smiley face. She spun it on the counter and laughed as it rocked back and forth, jingling. "Jessie will love this."

Simple pleasure. Rick had never met a woman who got so much joy out of the simplest things. He supposed part of the attraction was her optimism about everything. For too long he'd had little to lift his own spirits. After a moment of hesitation, he idly wandered to the playpen. On her back, her arms and legs moving, Jessie curved her bow-shaped mouth into a grin.

Instinctively Rick smiled back. "You're a charmer, aren't you?"

As if answering him, Jessie gurgled.

"She's flirting," Mara informed him. "She loves deep voices and—" She halted herself. He was being polite, nothing more. He wouldn't be interested in a mother's gushing about her baby. Then she saw the sparkle of humor in his eyes. They were what she'd noticed first about him. They were a cool blue that warmed when he smiled. When she'd first met him, she thought that they appeared a touch sad.

Rick crossed to a stool by the counter. He viewed the playing cards spread on the coffee table. With so many people in her life, it seemed odd that she occupied her time the same way he did, playing solitaire.

"If I remember right, no milk or sugar?" With a look back for his response, Mara grinned. "I cheat," she said unabashedly about her card playing. She slid the cup of black coffee across the counter before dropping to the stool next to him.

"Doesn't everyone?"

Mara laughed but wasn't unaware of his gaze sweeping over her wet hair. "You caught me at my best," she murmured and grinned, shoving a hand through her hair.

More than once, he mused, recalling the night the baby had been born. She may think differently, but he'd thought that night was one of those times, too. The inner strength she possessed had amazed him as much as he admired her ability to laugh at herself now. "You have a great apartment." For some reason he felt more comfortable here than in his own place.

"I've lived here for three years, and my family is only a few blocks away. Actually, this is the neighborhood I was born and raised in," she said, almost proudly. "So I'll probably stay."

The comment told Rick that she liked stability.

"And it's close to my family's restaurant." The kitchen felt warmer to her, seemed quieter. "I work there. Well, I did before Jessie was born, and I'll go back in a couple of weeks," she added, before swinging off the stool and rounding the counter to grab a bag of doughnuts that her mother had dropped off yesterday. Setting three chocolate-covered crullers on a plate, she was aware her hand wasn't as steady as she would have liked.

Rick narrowed his eyes, certain he'd gotten a glimpse of nerves. "You're going back to work so soon?"

"I need money to support Jessie and me."

What about the father? Rick wondered not for the first time. Deadbeat dads irked him. Too often while in foster homes when young, he'd met some kid who'd pulled the same fate as him because the mother, alone and without a good education, had been left holding the bag financially and had to care for her children. In all things, Rick believed that a person should bear responsibility for his actions. Sipping the coffee, he didn't state his opinion. As much as he empathized with her problems, they were none of his business.

"Anyway, I'm lucky in comparison to some new mothers." Lazily Mara returned to the stool. "I'll be able to take Jessie to work with me." Tired of the sound of her own voice, she sent him an inquiring look. "Where are you working?"

Rick assumed there was no way to avoid answering a few questions. "Bowman's Garage."

"I believe it's good if you like what you're doing. Do you?"

Rick felt her demand for eye contact. "I like it." Though he hadn't given that a lot of thought, he realized he did like the job and the work. The mechanics at Bowman's Garage were a good crew, quick with jokes and easy at accepting a new man. "I do a lot of the diagnostic work."

Humor rushed into her voice. "Sort of like playing sleuth, isn't it?"

Rick couldn't help grinning. "I guess so. I never thought of it that way."

Urged on by the hint of a smile, she chose innocuous conversation that would keep him relaxed. "I love the old mystery movies. You know, Charlie Chan and the ones with Dick Powell and Myrna Loy. The *Thin Man* series."

This time he did smile. If a relationship didn't work out, he would like a friendship with her. As it stood, he wasn't sure he could manage only that if he didn't stay clear of her. "Did you ever read any of Dashiell Hammett's other books?"

"Everyone has read *The Maltese Falcon,* haven't they?" she answered easily but her mind raced. She realized how much intelligence existed in his face. Of course, looks were no indicator of IQ. But she wondered, not for the first time, who are you? Years ago she'd gone out with a mechanic. The only thing he'd ever read were hot-rod magazines. That Rick was perusing her bookshelf provoked another question. "Do you like Tennyson?"

"Robert Frost," he answered before taking another sip of coffee.

Mara didn't prod. By his cut-and-dried answer, he'd indicated she'd already asked too much. "I've been told I have a tendency to ask too many questions. It's not nosiness. Really," she insisted, wanting him to believe her. "But how can you talk to someone if you don't know anything about that person? So if I'm bothering you—"

More than she would ever guess. More than anyone he'd met in the past year, she made him want to kick back and talk freely to her.

"My family says I chatter. But I'm used to a lot of people around me, so it's difficult not having someone to talk to, though Jessie is a captive audience." Her voice trailed off, her stomach knotting under the thoughtful gaze he leveled at her. The look was undeniably sensual. "And the weather has kept us in. I'm going stir-crazy." Self-consciously, Mara raised her cup as a shield. *Stop looking at me like that,* she wanted to say.

"Consider yourself one of the lucky ones."

"You don't like winter?" She felt him firing up something within her she wasn't prepared for.

"I'm not crazy about freezing my...backside." He shrugged. "Or shoveling snow."

To her, that seemed like an odd attitude for someone who'd moved from Texas to Chicago in the middle of winter.

"Are you going to answer it?"

"Answer—" She broke off as he cupped a hand under her chin and angled her face toward the ringing phone.

"The telephone," he said softly, letting his fingertips linger on her cheek.

Mara fought for a breath. His touch was far lighter, far gentler than she'd expected. It took another second to mentally snap herself back to her surroundings. Feeling foolish that her pulse was beating so fast, she twisted away and stretched across the counter to snatch up the receiver hanging on the wall. More unsettled than she wanted to admit, she amazed herself when she offered a steady-sounding greeting.

The voice that answered her purred. "Hello, Mara."

Mara mentally groaned. "Eddie." Bianca had given Eddie Romano her phone number a week ago. He'd visited her once and had been calling her nightly ever since. She wasn't thrilled. Plopping her backside on the stool once more, she visualized Eddie running a hand over the side of his slick, dark hair. Though her sister had thought he resembled Sylvester Stallone, he didn't even flutter Mara's heart.

Standing, Rick shifted his stance to catch her attention. "I'll leave," he whispered.

Eddie said something about a movie. Mara was too distracted. She held up a finger in a gesture indicating Rick should wait and cupped a palm over the mouthpiece. "I'll be done in a minute."

No amount of time mattered. Rick offered his back to give her privacy. He didn't want to stand around and listen to a cozy conversation between her and some guy.

With effort, Mara focused on Eddie again, wondering how she could keep the conversation brief.

Eddie droned on, raving about an adventure movie that newspaper critics claimed had an inordinate amount of violence.

"I'm sure it's great," Mara answered, even managing to keep a smile in her voice while she searched her mind for a way to refuse him gently. "I'm kind of busy right now," she fibbed to avoid hurting his feelings.

"Oh." He fell silent then cleared his throat. "Well, I'll give you a call again in a few days, and we can set a date then."

Mara said a goodbye and heaved a deep sigh. She needed to be less wishy-washy with him. If she kept worrying about sparing his feelings, she'd find herself trapped in a date.

At the silence behind him, Rick pivoted away from the window to face her. Discomfort shadowed her eyes.

"I don't want you to get the wrong impression." Her shoulders drooped noticeably. "I hate lying. I do. But that was Eddie. My sister, Bianca, decided he's the romantic find of the month for me."

And she'd been too softhearted to turn him down cold, Rick assumed.

Mara debated with herself about saying more. What woman wanted to explain to one man that another didn't make her blood warm, especially when the one she was talking to heated up too many feminine instincts?

Rick noted that she was deliberately avoiding his stare. He was used to observing people. They avoided eye contact when they lied or when they were worried they would reveal too much. Because he was tempted to touch the damp fringe of bangs covering one of her eyebrows, he grabbed his cup and drained the coffee.

"Do you want more coffee?"

What he wanted was for her to stop causing a damn tug on his insides. "No. I really should leave."

Mara didn't argue with him as he crossed to the door in a few strides. She was too susceptible, too vulnerable to this man. Seconds passed before she acknowledged he'd closed the door behind him. No goodbye. Nothing. Perhaps that was best. She seemed to be one of those women who was attracted only to men who weren't any good for her.

Or possibly, the vague interest in him was nothing more than a way to alleviate the boredom taking hold. She'd been truthful; she was bored silly by the weather. For sanity's sake, she needed to get out of her apartment.

As Jessie babbled, Mara hurried to her. At present, her daughter was the most settling influence in her life. Everything Mara did would affect Jessie. Everything. And that included bringing a new man into her life.

Rick left her apartment in no hurry to spend the evening with someone else. Still, he convinced himself that all he needed was a woman. For now, that had to be enough.

But the arranged date with Rhonda didn't help. In fact, it was a bust. Every effort Rick made to enjoy himself failed. She was a curvy redhead with a high-pitched laugh. He made polite attempts at conversation, even struggled to smile.

By the time he'd taken her home and returned to his apartment, he felt drained from working too hard at liking her. He'd had worse dates. He'd also had plenty that were better. But the biggest problem had been a yearning to hear another woman's voice. He'd listened to Rhonda and longed for Mara's softer, smoky-sounding voice.

He still did. But he could think of no excuse to knock on Mara's door at midnight.

Chapter Four

Rick reasoned that nothing would be more danger-ous for him than to get close to Mara—or unfair to her. He could end up leaving without a goodbye and hurt her, and himself. So it made sense to keep his distance.

He spent the next three weeks doing that, but she hadn't disappeared from his life. Though he left ear-lier in the morning for work and deliberately came home late, he caught glimpses of her going to the gar-bage can, rushing from the apartment building with Jessie bundled in her arms and hurrying into her par-ents' car.

Last night he'd looked out his living room window and seen her walking away with a curly, dark-haired guy. A muscle-bound, cocky type who had probably never looked over his shoulder in his whole life.

Ironically, Eric Lassiter never had, either. Rick Sloan, though, fought paranoia. So badly that sometimes at night he would lie awake and relive those hectic moments when he'd been ushered through the dark basement hallways of a courthouse and had dashed for safety into a deputy sheriff's car.

The loneliness and the restless discontent had begun then. He missed the interaction with people most of all. To him, that explained the interest in Mara. He wanted to believe she was nothing special. He was simply lonely.

Obviously the rest of the tenants believed that, too.

His landlord's wife, Beatrice Torrence, had knocked on his door often to present him with another plate of chocolate-chip cookies or a casserole dish filled with beef stew and a claim she'd cooked too much. Then a dapper-looking senior citizen who'd identified himself as Mr. Weisman had cornered him on the stairs and plunged into conversation for half an hour about the city's hockey team. A younger couple on the first floor had a nine-year-old son who lived and breathed football. More than once when Rick had arrived home, Andy had thrown a pass to him. And a frail-looking woman known as Mrs. Osgood had whiningly conned him into grocery shopping for her. In return, she'd knitted him a wool cap.

And something strange began to happen to him. For the first time in a year, he was beginning to feel comfortable with his surroundings.

* * *

Winter in Chicago at its worst, Mara reflected as she perched on the window seat and stared out the living room window of her apartment. Days of gray sky had passed. Soft fluttering snowflakes danced in the air. For weeks, icy sidewalks and streets had kept her indoors with Jessie. But the weather wasn't responsible for her dissatisfaction this morning.

Mara resumed pacing her kitchen now that Jessie's morning hunger had been satisfied. With a difficult task ahead of her, she grappled to think about something other than the phone call she needed to make.

For a Saturday morning, the apartment building was unusually quiet. She'd heard no movement from across the hall, either, and wondered if Rick was sleeping late. She'd heard him come in when she was giving Jessie her midnight feeding. Then she'd wondered how he spent his evenings—where he went, what he did, who he was with.

Since the evening when he'd delivered the package, he'd made himself absent from her life. She told herself to be grateful. Instead she felt mystified, not by him but by herself and the time she'd spent thinking about him.

This morning she believed it was nothing more than an avoidance ploy to dodge what really bothered.

With Jessie snug in her crib, she had the time to make the phone call she was dreading. Irritated at her cowardly streak, she grabbed the telephone, drew a few of the deep breaths that were guaranteed to relax a person, then punched a long-distance number.

After several rings, only pure willpower made her clutch the receiver and wait. Her apprehension intensified as she heard a hello. "Roberta, it's Mara," she said and hated the strain even she could hear in her voice. Silence followed for so long that Mara wondered if her sister-in-law had hung up. "Do you know where Steve is?"

"No," Roberta Denzloe answered in a tight tone. "Mara, he isn't here anymore. I told you when you called before that he'd been here for a few weeks, but I haven't seen him since."

Mara hated confrontations of any kind, but she had no choice this time. "Roberta, I can't believe your brother hasn't contacted you."

"Well, he hasn't. I told you before if he calls me, then I'll tell him about the baby." Her sister-in-law's voice rose. "Why don't you quit the concerned-wife act, Mara? You don't care where Steve is. What you want is child support."

Mara struggled to keep control on her frustration.

"You know—" Roberta paused. "You know, Steve could get a lawyer, too."

Mara coiled the telephone cord tightly around a finger as her stomach somersaulted. Steve didn't care about Jessie, didn't love her, or he would have wanted to see her by now. Roberta's comment was meant to manipulate. Mara hated power plays. They reeked of dishonest feelings and motives. Somehow she quelled the urge to slam down the receiver.

"Think about that," Roberta said quietly.

A dial tone suddenly resounded in Mara's ear. As if a chilling wind had blasted into the room, she shook with anger and eyed the stack of bills on her kitchen counter, bills made by Steve and left for her to pay. He always had to have the best of everything.

"For image, Babe," he'd said. "I have to look successful to be successful."

Her shoulders drooping, Mara plopped on the sofa. She felt drained from the brief conversation and had to wrestle for a bright-eyed smile when her mother arrived five minutes later.

She studied Mara at length before crossing to the kitchen to set a plate covered with aluminum foil on the counter. "Bianca said you went out with Eddie Romano last night."

"He struck out," Mara answered while pouring coffee.

Her mother paused in removing her coat. "Should I ask why?"

Mara lifted a corner of the foil and peeked at the fruit-filled coffee cake. "He's in love with his muscles."

Her mother laughed. "He does have enormous ones, doesn't he?"

Mara arched an eyebrow. "Does Papa know you're ogling other men?"

"Phooey. There is no man for me but your papa."

While she disappeared into the bedroom to see Jessie, Mara cut several slices of the coffee cake.

"She's sleeping like a little angel," Teresa said, ambling back to join Mara at the kitchen table.

"This is wonderful," Mara mumbled around bites.

Her mother heaved a sigh. "I suppose I should tell you why I came."

Mara sent her mother an amused grin. "To see both of us?"

As expected, she took the tease in stride. "Yes, but I'm also here because your papa met a young man last week who—"

Mara didn't let her finish. "Mama, I don't want to go out with him."

"He's really a nice man, a teacher. I know how much you like the intellectual type."

Though Mara maintained her best stubborn expression, she knew it usually had little effect on her mother. "I'm not ready for a new man in my life."

Concern suddenly crept into her mother's voice. "You're not still in love with Steve?"

Mara directed a you've-got-to-be-kidding look at her. "He killed any love I ever had for him."

The worry etched into her mother's forehead deepened. "Are you letting what happened with him— well, what is it, they say? Burned once and never again, or something like that."

Mara thought her mother must have been adorable in her youth. "No, don't worry. It would be silly if I let one bad experience influence my life forever. But I really couldn't deal with more than friendship right now."

"I see."

Mara searched her mother's eyes. She wondered what would convince her family that she wasn't husband hunting. Before she'd had Jessie, she'd decided that she and her daughter would do fine alone. "Do you?"

As if to emphasize her understanding, she gripped Mara's hand. "Yes, I really do. But I don't believe Papa or Bianca will give up."

Mara shrugged slender shoulders. "At least you're in my corner."

"Your brother is, also," her mother assured her.

Mara discerned, though, that Nick believed she was too compassionate, too kindhearted, too easily fooled. Unfortunately, Steve had proven Nick right. Her ex-husband had bamboozled her royally. "I called Roberta." She quickly filled her mother in on the phone conversation.

Her mother reacted predictably. "She lies as well as her brother does." She clucked her tongue. "I can't understand how he can ignore news about his own daughter."

"I know the way he thinks. If he doesn't acknowledge Jessie, she doesn't exist."

Though her mother made no comment, she shook her head in disbelief. "Eat some more coffee cake," she urged instead. "And for lunch I'll make ricotta pancakes."

Food was her mother's solution to all stressful situations.

The phone rang. Mara purposefully put a bright smile in her greeting and was glad she did when Bianca responded to it.

As usual, her sister drilled her with questions about Jessie.

Mara suspected Bianca's delight for her was dulled by her own unsuccessful attempts to have a baby, though she would never admit to anything but joy over

Jessie. "Are you hinting you want to come over?" Mara finally asked when Bianca took a breath.

"I thought you'd never ask."

Smiling, Mara set down the receiver. In answer to her mother's inquiring expression, she repeated Bianca's twenty questions.

"Such a curious child, she was."

"Nosy is a better word for it," Mara commented on a laugh, watching her mother remove knitting needles and unravel pink and white yarn from a large canvas handbag.

"She means well."

"I know she does." Mara's smiled waned. "Do you think she's handling this all right?"

Teresa nodded. "She's fine. She loves Jessie. But I worry about her. Six years of doctors. Too many tests. And always she's checking her temperature and counting days."

"They want a baby badly." Mara offered what she'd heard. "Angelo said he's been discussing adopting with Bianca."

"That would be good." Teresa waved her hand. "Since I'm here and can care for Jessie, why don't you take a walk?"

Still tense from the conversation with Steve's sister, Mara needed no further encouragement.

Sliding on her gloves, she dashed down the stairs. The instant she stepped outside and the crisp air tingled her face, she thought of a better way than a walk to handle nervous energy. It took less than a few minutes to round up a snow shovel from the basement.

* * *

Stepping from his car, Rick bowed his head against the onslaught of snowflakes greeting him. He was beginning to think winter would never end. He closed and locked his car door. Then he noticed her.

Head bent, as if on a mission, Mara rhythmically scooped snow from the sidewalk. He imagined the weight of the snow on the shovel. He also remembered how delicate she'd felt when he'd carried her in his arms. "What are you doing?" he asked from feet away.

She swung a look back. It hadn't been necessary. He had a distinctive voice. Low, a touch raspy, it could sound soft and buttery, or rough like sandpaper.

"You just had a baby."

That he felt the need to remind her of that fact stirred her grin. Leaning on the shovel, Mara raised a face glowing from the cold. "That was weeks ago."

To Rick, it seemed like yesterday when she'd knocked on his door, wincing in pain. "Why isn't someone else doing this?" he asked and blocked the path of the shovel.

"Ernie usually does," she said, referring to the building's maintenance man. With a shift of her body, she resumed scooping snow off the sidewalk to the right of him. "But he had to drive to Beloit to see his sister. She had an emergency appendectomy, and by the time he gets back tonight, there could be another foot of snow."

Rick migrated to his right, halting her, and nearly yanked the shovel from her. "That still doesn't answer why *you're* doing this."

Mara took another breather from the task, growing annoyed by his interference when she was trying to get the chore done before she froze. "Because the sidewalk needed to be shoveled."

Rick acknowledged that her slenderness deceived. With a tip of her chin, she revealed iron-willed determination that contradicted her fragile appearance. She set her mouth in a firm line. Dashed with color, her lips looked inviting. Would one kiss satisfy him? he wondered. Would thoughts of her stop intruding into his life, if he had one night of passion with her? Just one night. In defense against his own fantasizing, he drew back.

Mara heard his muttered oath before he spun away toward the walkway that led to the back door. Puzzled, she shook her head then resumed the task at hand. On every occasion, he'd left her feeling the same way—baffled or unsteady.

With the crunch of footsteps on the snow behind her, she lifted her head to see Rick approaching with another shovel.

"I'll finish," he insisted.

She raised her chin a notch. "If you want to help, then fine," she said, aware she didn't sound too grateful. Her breath puffed on the freezing air. She needed to keep shoveling, to work out rarely felt irritation directed at her sister-in-law, at Steve, at the whole situation.

"You're stubborn."

Mara blinked against the snow dusting her eyelashes. "You, too," she said more quietly. He didn't deserve to be the recipient of her foul mood, she reminded herself.

For a few seconds the only sounds were their shovels scraping the cement. Snow rushed down around them, laying a thin sheet of white on the sidewalk already shoveled. The wind hurled flakes from the ground up at them.

Head bent, Rick hunched deeper in his jacket to resist a chill and scooped snow that she'd missed. "You're nuts to do this if you don't have to."

Slightly winded from the cold air in her lungs, Mara paused, barely stifling a giggle. She doubted he'd given much forethought to his comment. "Seems to me you are, too, then." As he slanted a withering glare at her, she watched the breeze tousle his fair hair.

"Where's the baby?" he asked, though he doubted she would do something dumb and leave Jessie alone.

"My mother is visiting with Jessie." Her back aching a little, she stretched. "Did anyone tell you about the potluck dinner next week? It's at the Valquez's apartment. We have one once a month, different apartment, different food. It's a tenants' meeting."

Rick followed her shift in conversation. "To keep the landlord on his toes?"

"Something like that." A vague smile bracketed a smile line at the corner of his mouth. She liked the way his lips curled up on one side before a smile fully formed. And she'd always been drawn to brooding eyes. While she would never deny his attractiveness, she was too sensible to let a man's looks blind her to his flaws.

She was sure he had his share of them. He must have. But what were they? Except for being rather solitary, even secretive, she couldn't name any. To her, he'd shown kindness. He'd gone beyond neighborly duty by staying with her in the hospital. He'd held her hand. He'd soothed her. He'd shown only thoughtfulness. "Think about it. There will be plenty of food."

"Maybe."

Silence hummed in the air between them. Mara saw something potent in his eyes, a need that she couldn't read, but she felt it drawing her to him. She didn't want this, she told herself. She really didn't. She was still reeling from the failure of her marriage. She couldn't handle anything more serious than friendship.

What he'd felt from the beginning was on Rick again. It was nuts. As cold raced a chill through him, heat sprang up inside him. "Are you cold?"

Warm. Incredibly warm. She couldn't ignore the jolt she felt every time he looked at her.

Then he touched her. With ungloved fingers and a touch as light as a butterfly's caress, he brushed back strands of her hair blown forward by the wind. Like a strong, gripping magnet, the sensual pull tugged at her. Her stomach fluttered at the caress of his fingertips grazing the sensitive flesh near her jaw. Instead of a cold touch, his hand felt icy hot against her skin.

"Are you?" he repeated and tugged her scarf up higher around her neck.

"No." Soft. His voice carried that soft, lulling quality. She stepped back and let out a rush of air, not realizing until that second that she'd been holding her breath. In more ways than one, she'd moved away too late.

With a sigh, Mara spotted her sister plowing through a snowdrift at the curb. She also saw Bianca's curiosity. How much had she seen? Mara wondered. Could she tell that her little sister had been a fraction of a second away from leaning into the man before her, from urging him to kiss her?

Mara needed no mind-reading abilities. Even before Bianca reached the snow-cleared sidewalk, her eyes darted from Mara to Rick. Like some general leading his troops to battle, she stomped through knee-high snow to move closer to them. "You got here quickly," Mara said lightly.

Frowning, Bianca gestured in Rick's direction with a sideways movement of her head.

With little choice, Mara followed her cue. "Bianca, this is Rick Sloan, my neighbor."

Bianca gave him a quick, squinty-eyed stare. "It's good to meet you."

Rick offered a short "Hi," then lowered his head.

Mara knew his reticence was as good as waving a red flag in front of Bianca. Certain that questions were flooding her sister's brain, Mara rushed in, "Mama is already here. Why don't you go upstairs."

Bianca's probing stare shifted from Rick back to her. "Aren't you coming up, too?"

"In a while."

Rick caught Mara's arm to take the shovel from her. The sister was too curious for his own comfort. "You go in."

She didn't want to go inside. She wanted to let the crisp air caress her skin. Inside her apartment, she would feel smothered by more than the building's heat. She would be grilled with questions. But she set the shovel against the banister even as she dreaded the moments ahead. Maybe she could avoid some of them, she reconsidered. Her family's nature leaned toward spontaneous invitations to friends and neighbors. If she treated him as expected, that might dissipate some of her sister's inquisitiveness about what she'd seen. "Why don't you stop in for coffee when you're done?"

His head bowed, Rick warred with himself, wanting to say yes. A dumb thought. Already he knew that too much closeness with her promised trouble.

He kept shoveling. He wouldn't come—couldn't. "Some other time," he answered. Without looking up, he sensed the sisters had started up the steps. He scraped the last of the snow and straightened. Time and distance from her hadn't helped.

Unbelievably, Bianca made no mention of what she'd witnessed, and Mara managed a relaxing lunch with her mother and sister, then fed Jessie. Content, her daughter entertained them, delighting her grandmother and aunt with her quick smiles and garbled sounds.

Feeling too complacent was sometimes a giant mistake, Mara decided. For when their mother left for home at six to make dinner, Bianca remained on a counter stool as if glued there.

They watched a mystery on television and five minutes of the news before Bianca said without preamble, "Your new neighbor is too quiet."

Mara thought Bianca had shown enormous restraint, waiting as long as she did.

"And what was going on out there?"

Still in no mood for a discussion about Rick, Mara roamed the living room, picking up a blanket and a few toys. "We were shoveling snow."

Not looking at all convinced, Bianca trailed her. "I know you went out with Eddie. Didn't you enjoy your date with him?"

Mara saw no point in pretending. She waved a hand dismissively behind her. "He took me to a boxing match."

On a groan, Bianca pulled a face. "I expected better from him."

Mara hadn't. Eddie was thirty-five years old, never married—and self-centered. Most of the men she dated were usually that way by choice. They didn't want involvement, especially with a woman who had a child, and her daughter was her whole life. As yet, her family hadn't steered any man in her direction who showed a real interest in Jessie.

"What about Jerome, the teacher that Papa knows?"

"I haven't met him yet." Mara had little hope for her family's matchmaking. Love couldn't be arranged, and while marriage was hard enough with love, it was downright impossible without it.

Lifting her sleeping daughter from the blanket on the floor, Mara kept her thoughts to herself. With her family, silence was sometimes the best way to avoid more discussion.

Bianca had other ideas. "You might really like him."

Mara shrugged. "I—" A quick, decisive knock on the door cut into their conversation. "That sounds like the fuzz," she said on a laugh, feeling momentarily grateful for any interruption. She set Jessie into the eager arms of her aunt, then opened the door.

With a knit cap pulled low over his ears and the collar of his jacket shielding his neck, her brother stomped snow from his boots on the doormat outside the door. "Don't you ask who's there before you open your door?"

Mara rolled her eyes. "Come in."

He thrust a package of diapers at her. "Here. I thought you might need these." Nick sniffed the air. "What smells so good?"

"Mama made pancakes for us."

"I haven't had dinner yet. Any left?" As Mara nodded, Nick whipped off his knit cap and shrugged out of his jacket, indicating he planned to stay for a while.

Helpful as ever, Bianca waited only until he'd slouched on the sofa before informing him, "When I came, Mara was outside shoveling snow with that neighbor."

Nick angled a look at Mara. "Seeing a lot of him?"

"That was the first time in weeks. Usually he goes to work, comes home and watches television."

Draping an arm on the back of the sofa, Nick shifted toward her. "How do you know that much about him?"

"I have his apartment bugged," Mara quipped with a grin.

"Cute," he retorted. "Are you going to explain?"

"Explain what?" Mara reached for her sweater. "I can hear his television." Actually she heard his radio, too. Rick liked jazz and blues, B.B. King and Aretha Franklin. "Don't look so troubled. He keeps to himself a lot."

"Does he act like someone who's looking over his shoulder all the time?"

Bianca scooted forward on her chair. "Why would you ask that?"

"Guys on the run act like that."

Growing weary, Mara ran a hand over the tightening muscles in the back of her neck. A few moments alone would help ward off a tension headache. "You ask more questions than I do," she said lightly to keep the discussion from growing more serious.

Though a frown flitted across Nick's face, he followed her mood. "Impossible," he teased.

Mara noted the humor didn't reach his eyes. Not eager to spend time fielding more questions, she grabbed the moment to escape his and Bianca's inquisition. "As long as Jessie has the two of you doting around her, I'm going to do my laundry."

Nick said the obvious. "It's late."

Mara hefted up her laundry basket. "Ernie plays security guard at night and checks down there regularly. I'll be fine,'' she added. Quickly she stepped into the hall. Before she shut the door, she heard the beginning of Bianca's weekly lecture to their brother about him getting married.

Chapter Five

After being cooped up in the apartment by the chilly snowy weather, Mara thought any different scenery—even the gloomy basement with its network of pipes, tenants' castaways and dusty corners—would be a welcome relief.

She descended the basement stairs that led to the dismal room. At one end of the basement, locked cages that contained tenants' possessions lined a wall. A furnace separated the storage units from the washer and dryer and the Formica folding table.

Not foolish about a woman's vulnerability in a basement at night, she scanned her surroundings before she tossed a load of whites in the washer.

Turning on the portable radio she'd tucked at the bottom of her basket, she listened to a talk show while waiting until the first load finished washing. When the second load churned in the water, she groped in the laundry basket for a paperback she'd begun reading weeks ago.

Though it was past ten o'clock, Rick ventured out of his apartment and down the steps to the basement. Fortunately Bowman's Garage used a service to clean his uniforms, but a lack of clean socks and underwear forced domesticity on him.

Opening the basement door, he heard the soothing sounds of the latest pop singer. A time had existed when he would charge into unfamiliar places without a thought. Showing more caution now, he went down three steps and bent forward to scan the basement.

Legs dangling, Mara sat on the folding table with a paperback in her hands. Though she looked exhausted and fragile with her hair pulled back and caught by a huge barrette, she swung a foot in rhythm with the music. Moving quietly, he reached the last three steps before he hit a squeaky one.

Startled, she jumped and twisted around with a frown, her hand reflexively grabbing the small canister beside her.

"Easy," Rick soothed.

Impossible, Mara mused. Nothing was easy for her when around him. Honest to the core, she admitted to herself that an insidious attraction existed for a man she hardly knew, a man who was determined to avoid anything up close and personal. "You're quiet. I didn't even hear you come down the steps."

Rick could have told her that a man learned how to move silently when his life depended on that ability. "Sorry I spooked you." Once he'd spotted her, he'd considered not coming down the steps, but the idea countered the most important code he'd lived by, one that had been challenged since being a part of the Witness Security Program—facing problems head-on. So he'd kept descending the steps, deciding he needed to ease her out of his system once and for all.

Mara flicked off the radio while taking a breath to slow a quickened pulse. "You didn't." Not too discreetly he glanced at the crumpled pages of the paperback in her hand. She caught the gleam of amusement in his eyes. "Okay, I was a little frightened," she admitted.

Rick crossed the room, noting the lid on the washer was up. "It's not safe down here so late at night."

She seemed to have an abundance of protective males in her life. In answer to his comment, she raised a can of pepper spray. "I came armed."

While working at the newspaper, Rick had interviewed his share of women who'd had pepper spray turned on them by their assailant. "It's still not safe." Pouring detergent into the washing machine, he swiveled a look back at her. "Why don't you do your laundry during the day?"

"It's too damp to bring the baby down here, and I can't get anyone to sit with her then."

Rick eyed the dial on the washer, pushed it and nothing happened. Feeling dumb, he looked sidelong to see if she was watching him. She was.

"Need help?"

Before he could protest, she sprang off the table. "You have to turn this dial, then pull out," she said, reaching around him.

"Pull out?" Rick scowled at the machine. "Pull out?" He hated feeling inept. "Why don't they make them all the same?" he asked with an annoyance that had nothing to do with the intricacies of operating the washer.

Her soft laugh curled around him. "How would they baffle the male population then? I can't count how many of my girlfriends have met their significant others in Laundromats because the man didn't know how to operate the machine. Women are suckers for helpless males."

Rick slanted a look at her. Despite his best efforts, he couldn't block a smile. "You, too?"

With any other man, she might have smiled back, but he kept looking at her with the same intensity that had nearly swayed her into him before. She felt as if she was falling into quicksand, struggling against it when resistance only sucked her in more. "Sometimes."

Her heart hammering, Mara seized a quick breath and retreated to the table. When tired, the brain didn't work on all cylinders, and the imagination intensified, she reminded herself. She'd gotten little sleep last night. Jessie had slept from six to nine, taken a bottle, gone back to sleep for three hours and awakened screaming for another one. If she was imagining too much, it was because she was tired.

Rick followed her return to the table. He liked the way she walked, the fluid ease of her stride. He liked the sparkle in her dark eyes and the way her dark hair shone as if she'd brushed it for hours. Hell, he liked everything about her.

At the sound of rushing water, he dumped clothes in the washer. From the beginning, her sweetness and genuine friendliness had enticed him. She was sunshine and brightness. She was laughter and smiles. She was everything that had been missing from his life, he realized.

Resting his backside against the machine, he watched her yawn and noted she looked heavy-eyed. "Is motherhood tougher than you expected? It looks as if you had a week's worth of wash there."

Mara tucked up tendrils that had escaped the hasty pulling back of her hair earlier. "Believe it or not, it's only two days. Babies spit and wet a lot. But she's wonderful," she assured him with a bright smile. "Each day, she seems to do something new, something miraculous. Like this morning, she brought her hands together. I think she realized they belonged to her."

Mara eyed the rest of her unfolded clothes. More exhausted than she would admit to anyone, she had to prod herself to reach for a crib blanket to fold. "I knew it wouldn't be easy. But a baby is what I wanted most. Of course, when I visualized myself cradling my child, I imagined its father would be looking on adoringly."

"Are you bitter?" Rick prodded, not out of curiosity but out of a need to offer what she seemed to crave most at the moment—someone to listen to her.

Mara wanted to dodge his question, but she'd held back true feelings from her family to keep them from worrying. "I'm too much of a romantic for that to happen. I always wanted marriage and a family of my own. Only next time, I'll be smarter," she said with a forced laugh. "More cautious. I have to be."

He could see that she was still beating herself up. He wanted to soothe her, to lean forward and touch the line marring her brow. Though she strained for a smile, she looked in need of a hug. He didn't offer one. It was tough enough fighting an attraction to her. If he started to comfort her, more defenses might crumble. "Don't be so hard on yourself."

Mara raised her face. She already knew he was sensitive and kind. It appeared he was insightful, too. "Everyone was fooled by him," she admitted because she wanted him to understand. "My parents thought Steve was wonderful, my sister hung on his every word, even Nick, my brother, eventually started accepting Steve. And Nick's a hard sell. During my six-month engagement and through most of the year I was married to Steve, he deceived my whole family. They'd thought he was the perfect husband. He had a talent. He was a superb liar."

And a jerk. Rick recalled Carl's assurance that every neighbor had lived in the building at least three years. "You lived here with him?"

"Yes." Mara stretched across the table, and with her fingertips snagged a pale peach teddy. It seemed vital to keep busy to battle the quick resurgence of hurt stirred by discussing Steve. "Though he wasn't in town too much."

"Why not?" Rick let his gaze stray to the wispy and seductive-looking cloth. It played with his imagination.

"He was a salesman for a computer software company."

Mentally, Rick nudged himself to concentrate on what she was saying. "Smart?"

"In the wrong way." Instead of folding the teddy, Mara tossed it on the pile of clothes in the laundry basket. "Like I said, he was great at fooling people."

When the washing machine went silent, he offered his back to her and transferred clothes from the washer to the dryer. Mara dropped the paperback into her basket. She detested woe-is-me people and had come entirely too close to portraying one. "I guess I'll be going."

That idea suited Rick. He was becoming uncomfortable with the tenderness invading him.

"Well." Mara stalled a minute longer. When he didn't face her, she gave up and started to reach for her laundry basket. Spotting one of Jessie's booties on the floor by the dryer, she jumped off the table to retrieve it.

A sound—shuffling footsteps outside the basement's rear door—whipped Rick around. He'd been told that the exit door to the outside was always locked with a key, so a tenant wouldn't enter that way. He caught a shadow of a man, then lights died and the dryer hushed. Only his earthy expletive cut through the stillness in the dark basement.

"The—" Mara gasped as his hand clamped over her arm. With a quick, rough movement, he propelled her into the closest corner. "What are you—" Stunned and trapped between him and the corner wall, she pressed a hand to his chest to push him away.

Crowding her, his body jamming against her, he flattened a palm over her mouth. "Be still," he whispered close to her ear. "Just for a minute."

Over his shoulder, Rick narrowed his eyes and scanned the inky darkness. He had heard someone. He wasn't so paranoid that he'd imagined the sound of someone outside the door. If there was, it was tough enough to keep himself safe. What would he do about her? If anything happened to her, it would be his fault. He was aware of his hand at her waist, of her heart hammering against his chest, of the pulse at her throat scrambling against his thumb. Each quiet breath he drew pulled in the subtle sweet scent that had haunted him from the beginning. As much to calm himself as soothe her, he stroked her hair, but didn't look at her.

A second passed. No more. And lights flashed on, almost blinding after the mantle of darkness.

"Hey, anyone in there?" a male voice called out as the outside door flung open. The building's maintenance man stood no taller than five feet six. In his late fifties, Ernie possessed a cherub face and a wide grin. At the doorway, he stared with widening eyes at them, probably wondering about the coziness of the couple hugging the corner.

Rick drew back with a halfhearted grin meant to encourage such thinking. "We wondered what happened."

Ernie nodded slowly, looking more convinced he'd interrupted a romantic interlude. "Sorry about that.

I was checking the basement circuit breaker when I realized someone might be down here.'' He shrugged apologetically before backing out.

Rick waited until he heard the click of the lock, then looked back at Mara. Still tight in the corner, she appeared pale and bewildered. How could he explain the sharp twist in his gut that had brought back a memory of a friend who, because he was wearing his coat, had mistakenly been hit by a car? Or the cop he'd seen gunned down while protecting him. The same intense panic had surged through him minutes ago.

Free of his grip, Mara finally took the breath she'd been holding and wrestled for calm. What was that all about? Only one answer came to mind. Fear. His had transferred to her in an instant. Why was he afraid? Why was he so tense, so suspicious? What if her brother was right? Nick had great judgment, a cop's instincts about people. He thought Rick might be on the run. People leading normal lives didn't rush into corners when lights went out. Didn't go on full alert at the sound of someone approaching. They had no need to hide; criminals did.

Rick swept a glance over her, needing reassurance she was all right. Her startled expression revealed that the only one who'd frightened her was him. ''Sorry.''

''What's wrong?'' Instantly she cringed at how idiotic the question was. If he was a criminal on the run, she reasoned, he would hardly admit it to her.

Backing away from her, Rick wanted to forget the past moments but knew she'd expect some kind of explanation. He chose one as close to the truth as possible. "Look, I had trouble with a guy. He made me jumpy."

Fear that he might be in danger pricked her. "He's after you?"

Trapped by his own actions, Rick wondered how to steer her away from asking too many questions. "I doubt that. He doesn't know where I am." He sincerely hoped that was true.

Mara inched forward out of the corner. "What did you do to him?"

Walking a fine line between the truth and a lie, Rick chose an answer that bordered fact. "I caused him trouble with the police."

Amazingly a sense of relief floated over her. If he wasn't lying, he was the good guy. "And he threatened you?"

As she continued to squint, as if to see what wasn't visible, Rick dodged her concern with a matter-of-fact tone. "It happened a while ago, Mara. Forget about it."

"But you can't?" she persisted.

He knew of only a few ways to handle the moment and stop her from probing deeper. If he walked away, ignoring more questions, or revealed anger to halt them, he would fan her suspicions. "Sure I can," he said softly, choosing the simplest action to guide her thoughts in another direction. Lightly he cupped her chin and forced her to meet his gaze. "It's easy," he whispered, bringing his face closer to hers.

As he'd hoped, she revealed a hint of nerves, her eyes widening with surprise. But in an instant he knew that his plan to distract her had backfired. Temptation taunting him, he entwined his fingers in strands of her hair. The soft, silky curls coiled as if trapping his fingers. Something flickered in the dark eyes staring up at him. He realized she was filled with doubts. In his own way, so was he. While fate played a major part in his life and determined who he crossed paths with, he still controlled some moments. Desire came like a hard kick in the gut. And he didn't want to move away. Not yet.

As if she'd come to the same conclusion, when he cupped the back of her neck, she angled her head, bringing her lips a hairbreadth from his.

Without pressure, his mouth met hers. Mara knew she could have stopped him. He'd given her enough warning. But as always, emotions led her. She'd expected roughness. Instead, the lips on hers enticed, persuaded. The more his mouth slanted over hers, the more her lips softened beneath his. Heat sparked feelings she'd believed had been stolen by another man. She remembered now. She craved it all—the excitement of a man's mouth and of his touch. She'd forgotten how much she could ache. And she yearned with needs, with the desire to believe all that she'd left behind was so close at hand again.

As he deepened the kiss and his tongue sought the sweetness within, an urge for intimacy washed over her. More slowly, more thoroughly, he twisted his lips across hers. She recognized the danger building within her and still didn't pull away. She strained against him, feeling his heat and hardness. Too quickly. Everything was happening too quickly. But how could she stop what he was stirring within her?

Sweet. She was so damn sweet. Rick filled himself with her—her taste, her softness, her passion. At the moment, he wanted *this* woman—no other. He wanted to lose himself in her until he forgot everything, except her.

No longer uncertain, he was petrified. He'd kissed her with an intent to make her uneasy around him, to keep her away from him. And now with hunger closing in on him, with her mouth pleasuring his, he had only one thought. He didn't want the moment to end. And it needed to end now, or he might not be able to let her go. On an oath, he yanked away.

Though he broke the kiss, Mara's hands remained on his chest. Dazed, she muddled her way through a maze of sensations and fought the excitement pumping her blood. As heat sizzled within her, she was suddenly cognizant of how foolish she was acting. She was a mother now. She couldn't go with emotions on some whim, but she let out a little sigh, not feeling wise or sensible at the moment. "I'd better get upstairs," she uttered, breathing hard. She didn't give either of them a chance to say more. She skirted past him, grabbed her laundry basket full of clothes and scurried to the stairs.

Rick nearly called her back. Instead, he swung around and gave himself a mental kick for frightening her. And for kissing her. He had no business thinking about her. A woman with a child needed a man who knew where he was going, a rock-solid man in her life, not someone like him. He wasn't even sure where he would be next week.

For a long moment, Mara stood outside her apartment. Placing her hands to her face, she felt warmth. Were her cheeks flushed? Did she look as if she'd just been kissed? Because Bianca was inside, Mara waited in the hall until her heartbeat steadied.

Leaning against the door, she wondered if Nick was still inside, too. He had suspicions about Rick. Unfounded ones, Mara had thought, until Rick had acted so edgy in the basement. What if he was a fugitive? No matter how much longing he aroused within her, she had some doubts. What if Rick had an unsavory past and a questionable present? If her brother was right, she might be considered guilty of hiding a felon if she was with him too much.

No, he couldn't be one. He'd given her a logical reason for his jumpiness. But to discuss any of that with her overprotective family amounted to stupidity. Anyway, what would she tell them? That when the lights went out, he'd grabbed her, and then—oh, yes, then—he'd kissed her. That was hardly criminal, and mentioning anything to her family would only succeed in alarming them.

Yet she did need to think straight. She couldn't trust blindly. Having done that once, she would never survive playing the fool again.

Chapter Six

Rick squinted against the morning sunlight glaring off the passenger's window of Wes's Jeep. The sunshine tricked the mind into expecting warmth. Instead, an icy wind whirled through the city. Engines froze when temperatures dipped. All through the morning, the garage tow truck had been gone, the mechanics' stalls had been full and the coffeepot in the office had been repeatedly empty.

Expounding about his latest love, Wes drove his Jeep around a corner. "She's really a knockout."

Rick recalled a similar conversation with Wes two weeks ago. "Isn't she an aerobics instructor?"

"And dynamite," Wes sang back, exaggerating each syllable.

"Careful. You might lose your bachelor status with this one."

With an adamant shake of his head, Wes assured him, "Not me. No ball and chain for me. Ever. Buddy, that's a life sentence."

Rick had never considered marriage in his future. As a newsman, the story had always come first in his life, so he'd never known any long-term relationships. There had been nothing deliberate about that. He'd simply never had enough time to treat a woman, *the* woman, the way she deserved in a commitment. Still, he'd never thought of marriage as Wes did—confining, restrictive. Hell, there were other ways to be as much a prisoner as a man locked behind bars.

"Here we are. Like I said, this is a great place for lunch."

In unison with Wes, Rick climbed out of the car. Wandering toward the restaurant door, Rick hoped his stomach could handle more greasy food from some diner. For the past few weeks Wes had been introducing him to every restaurant within a mile of the garage.

As a customer opened the door of this restaurant, mouth-watering aromas wafted out to the street. It was then that Rick glanced at the name on the sign hanging over the window—Vincetti's. Above the laced café curtains on the wide front window, Rick viewed the inside of the restaurant and saw the Vincetti clan—Mara's mother manning the cash register, her father weaving his way from one table to the next, the sister and her husband seated at one of them and Mara giving a blond-haired woman a departing hug.

"Great food here," Wes assured him, watching the blonde now coming out the door. "Close to the garage, too."

Stopping feet from the entrance, Rick scanned the restaurant's customers once more. No one set him on edge. No one except Mara. In the middle of his workday, he'd yearned for something as simple as the sound of her voice or the musical quality of her laughter. He enjoyed being with her, talking to her. That she accepted him without too many questions amazed him as he considered all she'd been through because of another man. Instead of being wary of people, she seemed to offer unconditional faith.

And she made him feel as if he could belong. Nothing else seemed real when he was with her. Yet in truth, she was a fantasy. He couldn't give her what she needed most—honesty or promises. Thoughts of being straight with her were futile—and dangerous, for the more she knew, the more he would draw her into his world of uncertainty.

Wes sent him a puzzled look. "This okay with you?"

Rick could have said no. Instead, jamming a hand into his jacket pocket, he stepped forward.

With the faint coolness drifting into the restaurant, Mara sensed more customers coming in but didn't look up. A cleaning rag clenched in her hand, she stretched across a table to clear dishes. Disbelief lingered at what her friend had told her. She'd been delighted by Joan's visit, eager to play catch-up after not seeing her for months. All her joy had fled when Joan had dropped a bombshell. Her husband had heard from Steve.

"Mara, did your friend upset you?"

Why were mothers so intuitive? Mara wondered and straightened to face her. "Joan's husband had a phone call from Steve, Mama. He's in Indianapolis." *New state and a new start.* "He's engaged." Mara released a mirthless laugh. "We're not even officially divorced, and he's *engaged.*"

Teresa released an unladylike snort that spoke volumes. "How unfortunate for her."

It was like her mother to remind her of what was so obvious.

Mara laughed and hugged her. "Thank you, Mama."

"Mara," Bianca called from a nearby table. Before their mother returned to her position behind the cash register, Bianca sidled up to Mara. "Why do you think he's here?" she asked low and close to Mara's ear.

"Why do I think who is here?"

"Him." Bianca's head bobbed in the direction of the customers waiting for a table.

Overhead lights caught the sheen in Rick's fair hair. Mara wanted to look disinterested. In fact, with her sister's speculative stare riveted on her, she thought that was imperative.

"Is he here to see you?" Bianca attached herself to Mara like a Siamese twin.

"No, he's probably here for another reason." Mara had thought long and hard about that kiss and the passion it had conveyed. Deliberately she'd analyzed the moments before the kiss. He'd been sympathetic, but so had others since Steve had played havoc with her life. She'd sensed Rick was lonely, and so was she, but that wouldn't explain what she felt when with him. She couldn't even interpret her feelings with a simple term like friendship since she knew so little about him.

She was also far past the age of confusing desire with other emotions. She'd endured that stage of life in her teens, when she'd believed breathtaking kisses symbolized man-woman love. So she'd come to the conclusion that more than desire was drawing her to him. She just couldn't pinpoint what that was.

"Mara?" Her sister listed toward her as if about to learn a government secret. "What reason?"

Levity always helped, Mara reminded herself and went with a tease. "To eat?" In response to Bianca's scowl, Mara shot her a toothy smile, then resumed clearing a table.

Like a town crier, Bianca took off, scurrying to each family member to direct their attention toward Rick. A cousin, Tony, gawked before taking Rick's order. Mara's new neighbor had been discussed in depth by the whole family via telephone conversations. Papa offered a halfhearted smile as if teetering between a stern fatherly look and his usual beaming one for customers, and Bianca kept nudging her husband and sneaking furtive glances at Rick.

Mara zigzagged her way to the cash register. "Mama, come with me." Mara ushered her to Rick's table. "This is Rick Sloan," she said when he stood. She aimed a welcoming smile at him. It took effort to act breezy after a kiss that hadn't been.

"Miss?" A customer hailed from a nearby table.

Mara swung away and crossed to the man and woman to take their orders but heard her mother.

"Finally, we meet." Her mother's smile blossomed. "You took care of our Mara when she needed someone most. We can't thank you enough."

Rick wished he hadn't come in. The deception he lived with always proved hardest with people who reached out to him. He acknowledged the thank-you before customers lined up at the cash register, and Mara's mother hurried to them. He felt eyes on him. It didn't take much for Rick to sense that along with friendliness, the Vincettis also possessed an abundance of inquisitiveness.

He leaned back in his chair but felt restless. Blame it on the libido. All morning Wes had rambled on about Michelle, the aerobics instructor. Though he'd skipped details, he'd painted a picture of the previous evening's date as romantic with quiet music and candlelight. Rick excused his edginess to his own need for a night like that.

"Got to make a phone call," Wes announced.

Rick stifled a grin when Wes took off toward the telephones. He wouldn't razz him; he understood such preoccupation with one woman, too much so.

Mara placed her customers' orders and announced to her mother that she was taking her break. Ignoring family stares, she weaved her way to Rick's table, then settled on a chair across from him. She debated about mentioning the kiss, and decided not to. Instead, she motioned with her head toward a plate of cheese-and-spinach ravioli covered with béchamel sauce just set in front of him by Tony. "You have the house specialty."

Rick heard delight and pride in her voice. "It looks good." He broke off a hunk of the crusty bread that was delivered with the order. "Look, about last night."

He sounded so casual. How could he be when the memory of the kiss still tingled her? Mara wondered. "I never gave it another thought," she answered, pride demanding she appear just as unaffected as him.

Rick wondered if he should feel insulted. He sure as hell had thought about it. "How does it feel to be back at work?"

That he was suddenly frowning rippled a twinge of pleasure through her. "Great. I missed seeing everyone. And I was needed. My family was shorthanded without me." Mara leaned back in her chair. Being discreet was *not* a Vincetti trait, she mused, noting a vigilance by family members. "Do you feel as if you're under a microscope?"

"You're lucky to have them," he said honestly. He'd never felt that kind of devotion from anyone.

Mara had always believed she was. Recalling his comment about having only a cousin, she couldn't envision being as alone as he was. However, a drawback existed at being the baby in the family. Constantly she received unasked-for advice. "When I told my sister you were from Texas, she wanted to know if you talked like a cowboy."

Head bent, Rick chuckled. "Actually I'm from Montana."

She realized that was the first time he'd volunteered information about himself. "A small town?"

Amusement deepened in his eyes. "No streetlights. But good skiing country."

Though interested, Mara managed not to sound too eager. "I like to ski. I used to do a lot of it."

"Me, too." He carried fond memories of a holiday in Saint Moritz.

Her dark intense eyes prodded him to tell more. "Were you an only child?"

Rick saw no reason not to share bits and pieces about his childhood. "My mother died when I was born. And I don't remember my father well. I know he ran the town newspaper." He could give her this much about himself. "He was a big man with a booming laugh, but I didn't see a lot of him."

Mara sat back, sensing he had secrets. While that scared her, it also made her determined to learn more. "He died when you were young?"

"Six. He got pneumonia," he said between mouthfuls of the ravioli. "Foster homes followed."

Mara considered the sadness that must have overwhelmed him at such a young age. Instinctively, she laid a hand on his because opening an old wound hadn't been her intention.

"It wasn't so bad," he assured her, dodging memories he preferred to forget.

"How did you know what I was thinking?"

Humor sparkled in his eyes. "Mara, you're an open book."

And you're not, she decided as he slipped his hand free of hers. *Why do you always pull away?* "How did you get so interested in repairing cars?"

Rick reached for another piece of bread. "One of my foster fathers was a mechanic." Jake Blesoe had made him help at his garage. At the time, all Rick had wanted to do was stick his nose in a book.

She understood him a little better. He'd learned to be a loner early in life, but for some reason, she didn't think he was totally comfortable being one now. Propping an elbow on the table, she rested her jaw on her palm. "Do you . . . ?"

"Lord, don't you get tired of asking questions?"

Because he was grinning, she wasn't insulted. She returned his smile, but hers lasted only a second as she caught sight of the man entering the restaurant.

Rick scrutinized the change in her expression.

Her eyes narrowed on the door, darkening. He thought he heard her hiss, but a trace of amusement colored her voice as if she were torn between it and annoyance. "My brother is here. The great inquisitor."

Inwardly, Rick tensed. The cop. The overprotective older brother.

As Mara had expected, Nick headed straight for their table. Because she had no choice, Mara made the introduction. In disbelief, she watched the two men measure each other while exchanging a handshake.

Nick played big brother to the hilt, draping a proprietary arm around her shoulder. "I checked out Pop's latest."

Thank you, brother dear. Talk about another man in front of the one you were with was deadly for any relationship. Of course, her brother was probably counting on that. Mara gave him a killing look when he flashed her one of those dynamite smiles of his that had weakened female knees since he was in the sixth grade. "I'm not interested," she said through barely moving lips.

Bracing a hand on the back of her chair, Nick went on as if deaf to what she'd said. "He's had four jobs in the past two years. I figured you'd want to know."

The information meant nothing to her since Mara had already scratched Jerome from her life. "Why don't you go eat?" she urged.

"Think I will." He grinned, seeming satisfied with himself now that he'd delivered his subtle message. Anyone interested in his sister would be checked out.

As her brother rounded the counter and disappeared into the kitchen to make himself lunch, Rick drained the soda in his glass. "Guess your brother told you to stay away from me, too."

Mara arched an eyebrow before rising slowly from her chair. She truly didn't understand him. She knew when a man found her attractive, when a comfortableness existed. She knew sparks were smoldering between them, yet he kept pushing her away. Her palms on the table, she leaned across it, bringing her face within inches of his.

The flutter of her breath warmed him. Her eyes captured his. Rick felt the pull, as physical as if she were touching him.

"Bet I'll do what I want." She sent him a quick smile, then turned away.

Slowly, he released the breath he'd been holding. She weaved a path around tables to bend over one and pick up dishes. The denim of her snug jeans strained at her bottom. The bright yellow polo shirt emphasized the few sun-lightened strands in her dark hair. He watched delicate hands stack dirty dishes.

Her personal plate was full, but she never seemed to run out of energy, or because of tiredness, lose that ever-present smile, or what he'd now determined was a fighter instinct.

Though he'd kept to himself for the past year, he couldn't stay indifferent to her. With a look around, he noted he still garnered the Vincetti clan's interest. Worried frowns said more than a thousand words. They didn't trust him.

Balling his napkin, Rick pushed back his chair and looked for Wes, who was beaming as he sauntered toward him. That's when Rick noticed the newspaper left by a customer that was on the table across the aisle. One story focused on Frank Van, summarizing his involvement in drug trafficking, his conviction because of material witness Eric Lassiter and his appeal for a new trial.

Carl Ingram would call tonight with reassurances, and Rick would mouth expected responses. But they both knew it was only a matter of time, and he'd be on his way to Miami to testify at the new trial. And then he'd be given another identity. So whatever he'd found here would be part of a past that belonged to someone who didn't exist anymore.

* * *

Mara dodged family questions and pretended conscientiousness about cleaning up in the kitchen. She wanted to be left alone for a while. Why did he have to be the one who made her so aware she missed the warmth and companionship of a man?

Frowning and feeling cowardly hiding in the kitchen, she eventually wandered back to the dining area. As she expected, Rick was gone.

Bianca was scampering toward her. "Your date is still on with Marty tonight, isn't it? Or is something going on between you and the neighbor?" Her older sister was never content when she didn't know everything that was happening around her.

But Mara wasn't ready to confide in her family about Rick. How could she when she didn't understand him or her own feelings? Though she wasn't thrilled about tonight's blind date, if she spent time with another man, she might feel a smidgen of desire for him. Then she could write off emotions stirring for Rick as nothing more than loneliness, because to place another name on it meant even greater confusion. "Yes," she answered softly. "I'm still going on that date."

Rick had an obsessive nature, driving himself when he wanted something. The trait had been an asset in his career, aiding him in getting the newspaper job and in ferreting out details for stories. In regard to Mara, though, he considered that part of his personality a real flaw. Being obsessive about one certain woman definitely wasn't in his best interest.

Exhausted after a day of overhauling a motor and replacing a transmission, he rubbed a hand over his stubbled jaw as he climbed the stairs to his apartment.

He heard the downstairs buzzer three flights of stairs below him and the outside door of the apartment building opening, then clicking shut.

At the moment he didn't give a damn about who had come into the building. At the fourth-floor landing, he dug in his pants pocket for his apartment key.

The day's newspaper story about Van brought forth everything he'd been trying to forget—he was a hunted man with no future.

Again, Rick heard the buzzer below him, and a quick lighthearted exchange between several people.

"It's on the fourth floor," a woman said. Laughter accompanied her next words. "Yes, it is a long climb."

Rick recognized the voice as Mara's mother's. He heard a man's chuckle that he thought belonged to her father, and he heard a deeper, more masculine sound that was unfamiliar to him.

She had a good relationship with her family. She was lucky.

He planned to let her stay that way.

His key in the lock, he opened the door, listening to her parents and friend plodding up the steps. It would be best for him to be inside his apartment when they reached the fourth floor. But the click of another door stalled him.

Standing in her doorway, Mara looked...wonderful. His fingers curled over the keys so tightly they cut into his palm. The dress she wore was dark, short and clingy. Thin straps curled around pale bare shoulders. Creamy smooth skin enticed. He sucked in a breath as his gaze traveled downward. The cloth plunged at the front to the shadowed hint of her breasts, outlined them and caressed her hips. He wanted to hold her, to feel her slimness, her softness again. He remembered how well she fit against him, how during one moment while the sound of a dryer had droned on, he'd forgotten about shadows, about everything except her and the sweetness of her taste.

"I thought I heard someone out here."

Nerves. Rick heard them in her voice. "They're on their way up." In an almost desperate manner, he reminded himself that if he didn't stay clear of her, he would always have to deceive her. "Are you going on a date?"

His eyes, so serious, cut through the slim thread of resistance she'd gathered since they'd parted earlier. *You weaken me,* Mara mused. "This is another of the family's prearranged ones. Ever since I filed for divorce, my family has been giving me an overabundance of sympathy and unasked-for advice. They've been sending eligible men my way. Jerome, the teacher, was my parents' choice. Eddie was my sister's candidate. She thought his muscles would overwhelm me."

Rick held his ground. As before, the fragrance she wore teased him. He gave himself another second to absorb it to memory. When alone in his apartment, he knew the scent would haunt him just as the sight of her in that dress boggled his mind. "They didn't?"

"Hardly." Mara knew her quick denial had revealed more than she'd meant to. "He likes boxing and eating anything that doesn't require a fork—hot dogs, pizza, tacos," she added as an explanation. The sound of footsteps on the stairs and the quiet conversation about the weather between her parents and tonight's dream man made her aware that only seconds were left. "Marty Cranston is my brother-in-law's favorite. My brother even thinks he's all right, but that's only because they both like hockey, and anyone who does is all right in my brother's book."

Rick found something reassuring in knowing that he had common ground with her brother. "And tonight?" he asked, bracing a shoulder against the doorjamb. He wished everything was simpler, but from the moment he'd kissed her, he knew nothing with her would be.

Was he reluctant to end this moment, too? Mara wondered. She sure was. Nerves dancing at the possibility, she toyed with the tiny pearl dangling from her earlobe. "It's Marty tonight coming up the steps. With my parents. They're baby-sitting." As his eyes caressed her, he made her forget that she'd dressed for a date with another man. He made her feel as if she were the most beautiful woman in the world, as if she were special. She wanted to follow her heart, yearned to step out the door with him.

The heavy thud of footsteps forced Rick to glance over his shoulder. Tall, smooth-looking, with sandy blond hair, her date snatched a deep breath as if winded. "That's quite a climb," he said, grinning.

Puffing as he reached the top step, her father wore a greeting smile that slipped slightly at the scene before him.

Mara didn't notice her mother's expression. Her eyes darted to Rick. So quietly she hadn't heard him move, he'd crossed to his apartment door.

Without a look back, Rick closed it and set the lock. He needed to shut her out of his life once and for all. The guy in the hallway was the kind of man who belonged in her life. Someone who'd be dependable, someone—anyone but him.

Chapter Seven

Mara had a good time. Not great, but pleasant.

That description of her date failed to appease Bianca, who periodically asked more questions.

Mara placated her with assurances that he'd taken her to a nice restaurant. Yes, he was a good conversationalist, sort of. No, he hadn't been all hands. Yes, he mentioned going out again.

Then Bianca asked the big question. Would she go out with Marty again?

Mara shook her head, sending her sister away with an exasperated sigh.

Tired from being out too late, Mara did something rare for her—she watched the clock, eager to go home.

Twice she yawned during the walk from her family's restaurant to the car. Motherhood and late night dates didn't blend, she decided.

In need of groceries, she planned to breeze in and out of the store. No such luck. The store was crowded with too few checkers at the cash registers and lines too long. She felt weary by the time she reached home.

Dusk had come early, late afternoon sunlight disappearing behind heavy pewter clouds. As the wind blew at her back, she raised the collar on her parka. Within minutes she would be in her apartment, snuggling on the sofa and sipping a hot cup of tea. She gave herself the reminder as encouragement while bending into the car for Jessie.

Wiggling in her car seat, she stretched arms and legs, then pulled forward as if eager to be picked up. Rush-hour traffic had jammed the streets as snow dusted the ground with a fresh whiteness. Streetlights now shone dully beneath the haze of snowflakes.

While her daughter had been quiet in the grocery store, Mara assumed Jessie would squinch up her nose and wail for a bottle within minutes. Mara wondered if babies had some built-in clock that made them insist on being held at inappropriate moments. Dangling the diaper bag on her arm, she leaned forward and unsnapped Jessie from her car seat. With her cradled in her arm, she hefted up a grocery bag loaded with diapers and formula. Behind her, she heard the crunch of snow beneath footsteps but didn't look back.

Rick had been halfway down the steps and headed for his workout at the fitness center when he'd spotted her. Ignoring her dilemma had been impossible. He bridged the distance between them swiftly. All night and through the day, the image of her in that damn dress had bugged him. So had thoughts of her being with another man. No reasoning—nothing—countered the need inside him to be the one with her. He neared her now with one thought. He wished he'd never heard of Frank Van or the Witness Security Program. He wished everything was different. "Give the bag to me," he insisted, slipping the bag from her. "I'll carry it."

Mara wished she'd enjoyed herself more with Marty, with any man but the one in front of her. She sensed the rockiness of the road she might travel with Rick. Yet she knew she'd take the journey with him if he offered.

She noticed his glance at Jessie. She liked that about him. Unlike the Eddies and Jeromes and Martys of the world, Rick was aware of Jessie. "Actually..." Her voice trailed off as she noted a frown had deepened on his face, that his gaze was riveted on a man trudging through a snowdrift to reach the sidewalk.

From a distance, Rick observed the guy. With a shift of his feet, he shielded Jessie and Mara with his body, but he wondered what the hell he would do if the guy worked for Van. With a trained eye, Rick assessed him quickly. Slim and sour faced, the guy was tramping through snow in expensive Italian loafers. Rick relaxed. The idiot was too soft looking to be the kind to do Van's dirty work.

Feet away from them, the man cursed as his feet slipped on the slick sidewalk. He wobbled and regained his balance before taking another cautious step. "Damn," he grumbled. Through the thick lenses of eyeglasses, he peered at them. "Do either of you live here?" Again, he portrayed a tightrope walker, spreading his arms out wide to aid him in keeping his balance.

With snow flying at her face, Mara squinted. "We both do."

"I'm looking for Mara Vincetti. Do you know if she's home?"

Mara's smile weakened because his tone had held no warmth. "I'm Mara Vincetti."

The man planted his feet as if he were on a swaying ship and withdrew a card from the breast pocket of his overcoat. "I'm from the Bebberton Collection Agency."

Without a glance down, Mara accepted the card.

Shivering slightly, he swore again. "Damn snow." The scowl over his annoyance with the weather fixed on Mara. "The agency has sent you several notices."

Inner tension mushrooming within her, Mara curled gloved fingers around the card. "Those aren't my bills," she said softly.

It didn't take genius intelligence for Rick to gauge what was happening. She had secrets, too. And plenty of trouble, he guessed, feeling disgust with a man he didn't know for placing burdens on her.

Aware of Rick's stare, Mara couldn't mask her humiliation. It warmed her face despite the icy wind blasting at it. "My ex-husband made them," she told the dour-looking man.

Not appearing a bit appeased, he shrugged, and with a gloved hand he swiped at the flakes of snow on the lenses of his glasses. "Then they're your bills."

Mara shuddered more from the impact his words had on her life than from the chill in the air. No way could she pay all of those bills. For days she'd sifted through the mound of envelopes on her kitchen counter, wondering what to do, especially with the ones demanding payment immediately. "But he made them," she said, trying to make the man understand. "He wasn't even living with me when he made them."

"But you were still married when he charged these items. So you're responsible, too," he said calmly but emphatically.

Taking a deep breath, she stifled the frustration rising within her.

He stood his ground, not even blinking an eye. "They need to be paid. Now," he added.

"I've just started working again." Incredibly Mara managed to keep a polite edge to her voice. "I could have something for you by next Friday."

A flash of snide impatience drooped down the collector's mouth. "That's not my problem."

Tension for her coiling inside him, Rick brooded over the discomfort in her eyes. She didn't merit this trouble, but one selfish bastard had stuck her with his obligations. "The lady has a problem."

Though a head smaller than Rick, the agency's collector pointed a finger at him. "This isn't your business unless you're the husband."

"I'm making it my business," Rick said with a quietness that he knew was more intimidating than if he'd raised his voice. "Why don't you think of a way to help her out?"

"The only thing I know is that you need to pay something *now*," he said to Mara.

"Try again," Rick insisted, shifting his stance.

A moment passed while the man sized him up. "Okay, okay." Swaying back, he took a more charitable path. "But I'll be back next Friday."

Mara drew a shaky breath. Waiting until that Friday wouldn't really make a difference. She didn't have the money. How could this be happening to her? she wondered as she watched him tramp back through the snowdrift to reach his car. From early childhood, she'd been taught by conscientious parents that bills were paid on time, that a Vincetti didn't get buried by debt. Certain scruples had been instilled in her, Bianca and Nick. Honesty, responsibility, credibility. And having her problems aired in front of others had never sat well with her.

Rick couldn't keep his thoughts to himself. "That husband of yours was a real winner, wasn't he?"

Mara released a weary sigh. "I learned that too late."

Her shoulders drooped as if something too heavy rested on them. He discerned she was having difficulty discussing the problem. Like a whirlwind whipping around him, her emotions and her dilemma sucked him in. Rick lifted a hand to touch her hair but stopped himself. He'd observed her striving for strength during a moment when she'd been incredibly vulnerable, and though the need to offer some kind of comfort washed over him, he said nothing.

She had no choice, Mara realized. She would have to show her mother the bills; she would have to accept financial help. Her already bruised pride would take another hit. And why? Because she'd made a giant mistake in loving the wrong kind of man. She hated not having choices. The humiliation burdened her as much as her problem did.

Quiet beside her, Rick watched her struggling to unzip her shoulder bag while keeping Jessie close. At first he'd considered her actions a stall to avoid meeting his stare. It occurred to him now that she wasn't really thinking about what she was doing. Her mind was cluttered while she attempted to sort through what he conceived was a major problem. "What are you looking for?" he asked to gain her attention.

Mara shot a look up. So lost in thoughts, she'd forgotten he was near. How could she? She'd been dearly embarrassed in front of him. "My key," she answered and pushed forward a slip of a smile. She considered the juggling act ahead of her and sent Rick an appealing look. "Would you hold Jessie for a minute?"

It seemed like a small request since he couldn't do anything else for her, but he cast an uneasy glance at the baby. "You want me to?"

"Please." Mara flashed a stronger smile because he looked so uncertain. "You'll be fine," she assured him. "You're bigger than her."

"That's what worries me." Rick mumbled the obvious, "She's so little. What if I drop her?"

Mara grasped at the humor he'd unwittingly caused and raised eyes bright with amusement. "You look strong enough to manage."

"Dammit," he muttered low when she shifted Jessie to him. "That's not what I meant."

Ignoring his glare, Mara nudged the diaper bag with its design of pink and blue bunnies onto his wrist. "Would you hold this, too?"

While she rummaged in her purse for her apartment key, he looked past the groceries in one arm and Jessie in the other to the bag dangling from the arm cradled under Jessie's bottom. With Bowman's Garage nearby, it was conceivable that one of the mechanics picking up a six-pack from the store at the corner might drive by. He'd be razzed for days.

Clutching her keys, Mara slanted a smile at him. Despite his protests, he looked quite natural holding a baby. "I'll leave the rest of the groceries and take only this bag up," she said about the one filled with refrigerator foods.

Rick shifted Jessie slightly in his arms. She didn't stir, but the bottom of her bow-shaped mouth moved. She tugged at him with the same intensity as her mother did. Never had he expected he would be such a sucker for a baby. "It's slippery," he said as an excuse, then added, "I'll carry Jessie. On one condition."

At his gruff, I-mean-business-this-time tone, Mara raised a serious look to him. "What's that?"

"You carry the bunny bag."

* * *

He also carted groceries up the stairs for her. By the time he brought up the last bag, he was determined that he would set them on the counter and leave. He walked into the apartment to the sight of Mara sitting on a chair with legs tucked under her and cradling Jessie. From the other side of the kitchen counter, he viewed Jessie greedily sucking at the nipple on the bottle. It should have been easy enough to exit without another word. But it wasn't. Peering into a grocery bag, Rick eyed the abundance of fruits and vegetables in one bag. "You don't eat only rabbit food, do you?"

"I'm a Vincetti. It would be sacrilege. Do you cook?"

When working at the newspaper, he hadn't even owned a refrigerator. He'd had a coffeepot and a microwave. "Frozen dinners."

Mara wrinkled her nose in disdain. "You don't cook at all?" she asked while she dabbed at formula dripping down Jessie's chin.

"Does opening a can of soup count?"

Pulling a face, Mara tapped Jessie gently on the back. "Hardly."

Rick still hadn't moved. He knew why. He kept thinking how she'd looked last night—sensuous, stunning—all for some other guy's pleasure. "How was the date?"

"He did everything right," Mara answered. *Only he wasn't you.*

"So you found a winner?"

Watching him move around her kitchen, Mara tugged at her bottom lip. Why did he look so right in her apartment when other men hadn't? "I didn't say that." Jessie let out an unfeminine belch, but her eyes closed.

"So was the guy a dud?" he asked, wishing he could prod her to say yes.

"Divorced." Mara pushed to a stand and started for the bedroom with a sleeping Jessie. "Wait, will you?" she asked from the bedroom doorway.

Her request was ironic. He'd been waiting his adult life for a woman like her. He resumed unpacking the vegetables. Within seconds she joined him in the kitchen. "About what you said." Rick turned a puzzled frown on her. "You're divorced, too—almost. So why would it matter that he is?"

"I'm not divorced like he is." Mara shrugged out of her jacket and laid it on a stool. "Through the appetizers and salad, I learned how he met his ex-wife. During the entrée, he told me about every gripe he had about her from her squeezing the toothpaste tube in the middle to her washing a pink blouse with all his T-shirts." Mara tossed her jacket over the back of a chair, then paused at the refrigerator door. "Then dessert took us through the divorce, the custody battle, the alimony and the child-support squabbles."

She wondered if he was ever going to take off his jacket. Probably not. If he did, that might mean he was staying. Opening the vegetable crisper in the refrigerator, she grimaced at the sight of a darkened onion and plopped it into the garbage can. "The ride home included his postdivorce trauma. We reached the door and he said he had a good time. I said thank-you, and that was it.''

Grinning, Rick lounged against the counter. "I'm amazed."

Mara looked up from stuffing a head of lettuce in the refrigerator drawer. "About what?"

A deeper smile tugged a corner of his mouth upward. "I didn't think you could go that long without talking."

As the youngest child in a family, Mara knew how to take a tease good-naturedly. "It wasn't easy," she said on a soft laugh and looked down.

Unsuccessfully Rick veiled a smile. "Graham crackers?"

His tease hung in the air. "Do you have a problem with someone eating milk and graham crackers?" Mara asked, feigning a narrowed-eyed stare that had no effect at all on him, except to spread the smile to his eyes.

"A great snack. And at its best while watching an old movie," he admitted.

Kiss me again. With him so near, Mara yearned for it. She wanted to know she'd imagined nothing—that it had been wonderful. "*Charade* is my favorite. I must have watched that movie twenty-five times."

"What do you like about it?" he asked, handing her the box. As she took it, he fingered the hair brushing her ear. The strands glistened. In fascination, he watched a curl coil around his finger.

"You'll laugh," Mara said, struggling to sound calm.

It took effort, but Rick let the strands slip through his fingers. He thought she might be right. She made him laugh more than any person he'd ever met.

"Cary Grant was such a fake, a scoundrel." She skirted a few steps from him to open a kitchen cabinet. "At least, that's what Audrey Hepburn thought. Then she learns he's honest and everything she hoped he'd be."

"You like happy endings?"

"Always."

He could never give her that. He could never give her or her child what they needed most—a man they could rely on.

Mara held the refrigerator door open and took the carton of milk he was holding. "I've decided we need to even things out."

Rick considered what had already passed between them. Because of her persistent friendliness, he'd gained more than she might imagine. "In what way?"

"You keep doing things for me, and I'm used to paying my own way," she said, leaning back against the closed door of the refrigerator.

Frowning, Rick snatched up a bag to fold. "I don't want your money."

"I didn't plan to offer any." Mara slit her eyes and looked up at him. Financially she was scraping by. No doubt he already knew that since he'd witnessed her encounter with the bill collector. "But I owe you for that night you drove me to the hospital."

No way could he take payment for that. "The cannoli," he answered to sidetrack her.

Though amused, Mara planned to win the game of words that had begun. "But then you delivered my package."

"And you gave me coffee and a doughnut." He wondered how to keep her away when he was dying inside to pull her against him. "And you instructed me about how to use a washing machine."

"Yes, but you helped me by taking Jessie for me outside when I hunted for my keys."

By Rick's calculations, one kiss meant he was way ahead.

"See, I do owe you."

Curious now, Rick played along. "What do you have in mind?"

"Dinner." There. She'd done it. One of them needed to take a stand. A kiss didn't mean a lifelong commitment, but she felt it warranted something more than casual conversations and chance meetings. "I'd like to cook you dinner. I'm really an excellent cook."

Rick didn't doubt that. Delicious-smelling aromas drifted from her apartment and permeated the hallway practically every night. "I've gotten used to frozen dinners."

A spark of humor rarely seen in him made her remember the sound of his laugh. She wished she could hear it again. "Okay. I could microwave a couple of frozen dinners. But my grandmother's spirit would probably haunt me for committing a mortal sin."

A companionable warmth flowed between them. Rick felt its enticing power. It made him want to take walks with her, spend the day in front of a television set with her, make dinner with her. Do anything, as long as he was with her. "I gather Vincettis don't cook frozen dinners?"

"Not even my brother. We were all raised to know how to cook. So will you come?"

Rick stopped himself from leaning closer and taking her mouth. The need to feel it beneath his overwhelmed him. "What's this about? Why ask me instead of one these guys your family has found? Because you think I'm safe?"

Far from it, Mara mused. He'd rushed excitement into her life with one kiss, but this wasn't the moment to tell him that. "I'm not afraid of bringing a man into my life again." Though his eyes appeared like slits, she could feel their intensity. "And I'm not afraid of you."

Lightly, he framed her face with his hands and forced her to meet his gaze. "What makes you think you can trust me?"

The question was one she'd asked herself too many times already. "The truth?"

Did he have a right to expect it from her when lies flowed from his mouth? Rick wondered.

"The truth is I'm not sure I can." Her voice trailed off as his fingers slid around the side of her neck to the back of it.

"You shouldn't." Leaning closer, he brushed his lips across hers. "You know I want you, don't you?" Gently he nipped at her bottom lip, but the temptation was too great. Need whipped through him as his mouth took hers. With an urgency he'd neither wanted nor expected, he moved his mouth over hers to absorb the sweetness. The kiss didn't appease even

each other, though I thought Rick would never warm up to any of us.''

An understatement, Mara mused. "He's not an easy man to understand," she returned because Beatrice kept studying her a little too closely.

"Suspicious, too."

Mara paid closer attention.

"He acts skittish around the mailman, any strangers." Beatrice's forehead wrinkled with a frown. "Yesterday he was talking to Mr. Genelli, nice as could be. They were laughing about Andy sleeping with his football. Then, all of a sudden, a delivery man came to the outside door, and when Mr. Genelli went to answer the ring, Rick took off up the stairs without a goodbye or anything."

As Jessie fussed, growing bored staring at the cuckoo clock on the wall above the sink, Mara shifted on her chair to dangle a rattle in front of her. She'd almost forgotten Rick's actions in the basement, but Beatrice's words assured her that he was a lot more tense about his past trouble than he pretended.

"He is a nice man, though." Mrs. Torrence shot a sideways glance at her. "Ernie said he thought you might think so, too."

Mara sighed, certain Ernie was spreading tales about seeing her and Rick in a clinch in the laundry room.

In a motherly fashion, Mrs. Torrence hunched forward, setting plump forearms on the table. "I see a sparkle in your eye."

"Do you?" Mara deliberately sent her an amused grin.

The woman's smile slipped. "But you will be careful, won't you?"

For reassurance, Mara closed her hand over the woman's. "Very careful."

If only she was as confident as she sounded, Mara reflected. The problem was she was beginning to trust a man who puzzled her.

With a full day ahead, Mara tucked Jessie into a bunting when she returned to her apartment, then fished her car keys from her shoulder bag.

Outside, snow swirled around her and the coldness stung her face. Shielding Jessie from the wind, she cautiously maneuvered down the snow-dusted steps and inched her way to her car. If traffic wasn't tangled by the snowfall, she might be on time for a pediatrician's appointment.

She hooked the back safety belt around Jessie's car seat before she slid behind the steering wheel and flicked on the ignition. Instead of a steady purr, an ear-piercing screeching resounded in the air. Growing out of sorts quickly, she muttered an oath and turned the key again. Once more, she heard a shrilling squeal.

Rick came home early since business was slow. With too much time on his hands to think, he'd sat at the computer he'd bought months ago and concentrated on the story he'd begun writing in longhand during the past year. In the fantasy world of his mind, he could forget the reality of Frank Van's threats, and he could forget Mara.

Into draft three of his manuscript, he felt confident about the story's salability. He assumed, though, that all writers had to believe in their work or they would never put a word on paper.

Noise outside broke a thought momentarily. He ignored it, keeping his fingers on the keyboard. When he heard it again, he jabbed a button to save what he'd written and wandered to his living room window.

Looking down at the street, he saw Mara pound a hand on the steering wheel. Rick snatched up his jacket and headed for the door, recalling comments about Mara made by Mr. Weisman during the hockey game they'd watched together.

"She's a favorite of everyone's. We all wanted to lynch that ex-husband of hers, but he took off before we could get to him."

Rick hadn't encouraged him to say more about her, not when he needed to forget that she existed.

The old man had gone on without any prodding. "She's sweet. We all think so. She's helped all of us. She cooked dinners for me when my Esther died and baby-sat for the Genellis when Carla Genelli had to leave town to stay with her sister. She always does for other people. So it didn't seem right that she'd gotten hurt like that," he said heatedly. "You want a friend," Mr. Weisman said, pointing a finger in Rick's direction, "she'll be there for you."

Rick could hardly have told the man that he wanted more than friendship from her.

Mara popped the car's hood and mumbled at the engine. Hearing the bang of a door, she raised her head to see Rick crossing to her. No amount of reasoning or private little talks with herself countered the pleasure she was feeling.

His jacket unzipped, he stopped beside her and leaned forward, setting a palm on the fender. "Let me look."

After his warning and quick departure last night, she wasn't sure of his mood. Mara thought it best to pretend nothing had happened. For the moment, she feigned interest in the engine or whatever it was she was staring at. "When I turn the ignition, it sounds like a banshee's wail. Should I get Jessie out? It isn't going to blow up, is it?"

"Is the key in the ignition?" Rick straightened beside her but didn't move. He couldn't. Damn, it was on him again, everything he'd felt the night before. He wanted to toss aside his gloves and place warm hands on her face, to brush his fingertips across her mouth, and like a blind man feel the shape of it. He'd wanted to kiss her until neither of them were aware of the weather—of anything except each other.

"Yes," Mara answered slowly. He wasn't touching her, and she was aching to be held by him. He'd sent her a warning last night. But how could she heed it if he didn't explain why he'd delivered it?

In a quick move, as if someone had jabbed him in the back, he sidestepped her to slide behind the steering wheel. She truly didn't understand him. If she felt the sensual pull every time he was near, so must he.

As quickly as him, she rounded the front of the car to reach the passenger's side and opened the door. With a glance at him sitting behind the steering wheel, she shoved the seat forward to unsnap Jessie's car seat. A sound as grating as before shrilled in the air again. Though his expression was unreadable, his expletive sank Mara's hopes that a quick fix would send her on her way. She unsnapped Jessie's car seat before asking, "Is it bad?"

Rick met her stare in the rearview mirror. Even the seat between them didn't curb the need. All he'd been fighting from the beginning hit him—hard. It didn't matter that he couldn't afford daydreams about having a woman like her in his life. He wanted her in it. "You need a new starter."

Mara readjusted Jessie's blanket, tucking it. "The brakes feel mushy, don't they?"

"Yeah, mushy," he repeated, amusement tugging at him. "It's low on brake fluid."

Mara nearly groaned. More money problems. She didn't need car trouble, too. Frowning, she nudged up the cuff of her jacket to peek at her wristwatch. "I'm going to be late."

If she was patient, she might get the starter to catch. Or she might not. Rick removed the key from the ignition and dangled it over the seat to her. "Where are you going?"

"The pediatrician's office."

One look at Jessie's toothless grin and Rick was sunk. "Come on. I'll drive you."

The offer surprised her, especially since he already looked as if he regretted making it. Mara couldn't be concerned about his feelings or her own. Jessie was scheduled for shots today. A canceled appointment might mean several weeks' wait before she would get Jessie into the doctor.

"I hate to say this to you again," she said once she'd finished strapping Jessie's car seat in the back and snapping her own seat belt, "but would you hurry?"

She'd used those same words on the night he'd driven her to the hospital. Then, too, he'd thought, what else could he do but help her? He reasoned now that he couldn't leave her stranded if she had to take the baby to the doctor. Anyone would have done the same. Another lie, he reflected and turned the key to start the engine.

In the parking lot adjacent to the doctor's office, Rick slouched against the fender of his car. The crisp air chilled him. During moments like this, he longed for Miami weather. When he'd left the small town in Montana where he'd been born, he'd been eager to seek a warmer climate and make his name in the newspaper world. Both goals no longer existed.

At the shuffling sound of footsteps, he pivoted toward the double-door entrance of the doctor's office. Snuggling Jessie close, Mara hunched over her daughter and uttered soothing words.

"Everything okay?" Rick questioned, pushing away from the car.

Head bent, Mara moved past him to open the car door. "Fine."

Her strained smile and unusual silence bothered him, but he followed suit and remained quiet during the drive back to the apartment building. More than once he peered in the rearview mirror. Jessie seemed okay. Eyes closed, she slept peacefully. So what was wrong? "Is Jessie all right?"

Her head bent, Mara finally succeeded in her search through her purse for a tissue. "Fine. It was only a checkup, but she got vaccinations today." She blew her nose softly. "I hate seeing them prick her with needles." Actually, she'd nearly cried. Disgusted with herself now, she made a face. "I know it's for her own good. One part of me is very sensible about her having the shots. But I wanted to protect her from the pain."

Rick braked for a red light. "Isn't that natural for a mother?"

"I suppose it is. Logically I know I can't protect her from everything. She'll get hurt in a lot of ways. But until this visit to the pediatrician, I didn't realize how hard it was for my mother after Steve and I broke up. She probably wanted to protect me, too." Giving a quick sniff, Mara shrugged. "I know I'm being silly. I'm too softhearted."

As the light turned green, Rick pressed down the gas pedal. More than once he'd thought she was everything he'd always looked for in a woman. "I wouldn't call that a bad trait." Despite his assurance, he knew that her perceptiveness could penetrate the world of someone hell-bent on leading a secret life.

Mara stuffed the tissue into her shoulder bag. She was too easily fooled. Hadn't Steve proved that? Her brother had tried to warn her. Even before she'd married Steve, Nick had insisted Steve wasn't being straight with her. She should have listened. Nick was good at judging people, being able to tell if they were lying. Lost in thoughts, Mara raised her head to see Rick pulling into the curb in front of the apartment building.

Rick flicked off the ignition, then rounded the front of the car. As Mara finally stirred to lift out Jessie's car seat, he reached forward. "I'll carry her."

What little resistance to him that she still possessed fluttered away. No warning from him helped, either. For what woman didn't long for a man in her life who excited her with his kisses, who warmed her with his thoughtfulness, who made her feel special? To Mara, fancy dinners and charming words amounted to nothing. She'd had a handsome husband who'd wined and dined her and had whispered plenty of soft words in her ear. He'd also been unbelievably selfish and inconsiderate. Because of Steve, a man's actions meant far more to her than his words. "I'm glad I saw you today." She paused as Rick slipped a hand under her elbow while they climbed the slick steps. "We're having my parents' anniversary party at my apartment in a couple of weeks. No gifts. I'm inviting a few neighbors and some of his regular customers. Well, they're more like family than customers. Would you come?" she asked because she believed she'd found someone special, someone she wanted in her life.

Halting at the door of the apartment building, Rick combated a desire to accept. She had no idea how much he wanted to be with her—and with other people. He was living a lie, standing back from life. It was a strange position for a man who used to welcome change and new friends, who connected with strangers every time he'd written a story. But Carl's advice had dictated his life for the past year.

"Keep free of emotional ties," he'd lectured. "You don't know who you can trust."

By his silence, Mara guessed he was going to say no. He still held Jessie. As if it were as natural as breathing, he'd tucked the car seat under his arm and braced it against his hip, then opened the door for Mara. "The invitation to the party stands," she said when minutes later she was unlocking her apartment door.

Rick followed her in and chose a spot near the sofa to set down Jessie's car seat. Squatting before her, he found himself captivated. Her bow-shaped mouth split into a smile before she yawned. Something deep inside him, like pleasure, swelled, warming him. God, the kid was beautiful. He'd thought so before, but what did he know about babies? Nothing. They belonged to a different world than the one he'd lived in most of his adult life. But he knew now, what anyone could see when Jessie smiled. As dark eyes gazed trustingly up at him, Rick brushed a knuckle across her soft pudgy cheek.

This was dumb. It was bad enough letting the mother inch her way under his skin. He couldn't get hooked on the kid, too. He snapped to his feet, needing to get out quickly. He gave Jessie one last glance. Again, she sent him a crooked grin, and once more he wanted to smile. "I've got to go," he announced, too aware of the feelings that mother and daughter detonated within him. Too aware that the wall he'd erected was crumbling. "Give me your car keys."

Mara swung toward him. "My keys?" she asked, still holding them.

Impatient suddenly, Rick closed the distance to her and snatched the keys from her hand, then quickly unhooked the ones to the car. "You can't drive with the starter and brakes like that." He set her apartment keys back in her palm. "I'll get your car fixed."

Mara fought a rise of uneasiness. "Are the brakes that bad?" Her voice broke as she noted the seriousness in his eyes.

"Here." Rick shoved his own car keys into her palm. For one instant, as her delicate fingers met his, he ached. It stunned him that he wanted so badly to feel her touching him. "Use my car."

Uncertain what was happening, Mara released a quick gurgle of laughter. "I couldn't use your car."

"Take them." He fixed a furious look at her. "You're not going to drive around with Jessie in *that* car."

"Are you sure?" She fiddled with the keys in her hand. Despite his offer, he'd sounded irritated.

Filled with annoyance at himself, Rick lashed out, "No, I'm not sure. I'm not sure of anything when you're around."

Mara remained silent. She couldn't say anything. All her energy was focused on what he'd said. The eyes on her were intense and filled with restlessness—and desire. She sensed the war inside him. She'd battled one of her own enough lately.

"I wish you'd get out of my head." He muttered an earthy curse as a yearning to feel her against him, to pretend the entire past year wasn't real, enveloped him again. God, he wanted to spend more time with her. He wanted it desperately. "This is a mistake," he said softly.

With his mouth hovering near hers, she didn't want to think too much. She swayed into him as if drawn to the warmth of his body.

Rick watched her lips part, invite, and he went with what he was feeling. Lowering his head, he let his mouth meet hers—and linger. He felt the light pressure of her hand at his waist and pulled her closer. This time, not dressed in an oversize sweatshirt, he could feel how slim she really was. This time he savored, letting the lips beneath his tempt him. Soothe him.

Regardless of what his good sense told him, he'd thought of nothing but holding and kissing her again. He moved his mouth over hers, intending only to sample. But her kiss was too generous. It carried a message that matched the passion gathering in him. She made demands with her lips and her searching tongue. She fueled him, her hands roaming down and then up his back to caress his neck. Driven to taste deeply, he captured her breath inside his mouth. Desire throbbed through him. He wanted to lose himself in her. He wanted her as hungry as he was. Starving.

He might not be good for her, but he wanted everything possible with her. He heard her moan and dragged her closer. That she trembled pleased him. He could force the moment, but he wouldn't. He felt her breathing hard. He was just as breathless, and it hit him that this wasn't a passion he understood.

Lifting his mouth from hers, he stared at her lips, swollen from his kiss, at her flushed cheeks, at her eyes dark with emotion.

Desire haunted Mara.

He made her feel again.

He awakened emotion she'd been unprepared to meet again.

He made her ache.

No denial would work. Her heart had opened to him with alarming quickness.

Dangling the keys in his hand, Rick stepped away. "I'll bring your keys back tomorrow."

"Dinner will be ready at seven," she said, determined not to take no for an answer.

He paused at the door, a deep, serious look clouding his eyes. "You don't know what you're getting into."

Maybe she didn't. But for a long moment after the door closed behind him, she stood still. It's too late, she wanted to tell him. You can't pull back now. No, not now, she mused. How could she let him when she'd felt the heat rising in him just as it had in her? How could she let him when one—and only one—thought persisted? Whether or not he'd be an easy man to love, she was falling in love with him.

Chapter Nine

"Angelo has a bowling tournament. I'll come over tonight, and we can talk," Bianca announced the moment Mara strolled into the restaurant the next morning.

Here goes, Mara mused, knowing her answer would send Bianca's curiosity into high gear. "Not tonight. I'm having company."

Bianca's dark eyebrows veed with her frown. "Who?"

Unless she was rude, Mara couldn't dodge her sister's inevitable questions. "Rick."

As expected, Bianca trailed Mara to behind the counter. "Mara, he's a stranger. No one knows him."

"I do. I know enough about him." Mara poured herself a morning cup of coffee. *I know he's compas-*

sionate and thoughtful. I know he excites me in a way no man ever has. She'd felt comfortable with Steve, and from there, passion had grown. It was the opposite with Rick. Attraction, even desire, somersaulted her stomach whenever he drew near. And she didn't always feel relaxed around him, but she felt his need to protect her. The reason eluded her, but in her heart, she knew he wouldn't deliberately hurt her.

"Papa," Bianca called. "She's having company tonight. The neighbor."

Cradling the cup in her hand, Mara noticed she'd gained her family's full attention, including Nick, who'd suddenly appeared at the archway that led to the kitchen. "Everyone wants me to find a man again."

Nick scowled while he munched on a giant-size sub sandwich, though the clock showed only eight in the morning. Her father frowned. However, her mother, as always, offered words of encouragement. "Have a nice evening."

With her support, Mara believed she could overcome any family objections about Rick. And that mattered to her. Her family was important to her. She couldn't welcome a man into her life if they didn't like him.

After leaving work early, she dusted and scooted around the vacuum. With dinner started and the table set, she showered. While dressing, she allowed herself to consider a dismal thought. What if he stood her up? Because the possibility meant another poke at her pride, she countered it quickly. He'll come.

With a few minutes to spare, Mara carried Jessie down the steps to retrieve the mail, which hadn't yet been delivered when she'd arrived home. One envelope stuck out of her mailbox.

Mara ripped open the envelope and simply stared at the sheet of paper.

Rick padded in stockinged feet from his bathroom while tugging a polo shirt over his head. He could smell garlic and onions and a sweet buttery aroma. His stomach rolled in anticipation.

When he'd arrived at work this morning, he hadn't planned to go to her apartment for dinner this evening. But at lunchtime he'd found himself in a liquor store purchasing a good bottle of wine. Driving home from work, he'd made another stop. It was then he realized how close he was to losing the battle with himself to stay away from her.

Now, with the bottle of wine dangling from one hand, he curled his fingers around the stems of the springlike bouquet that he'd bought. A woman like Mara deserved long-stem roses and romantic candle-lit dinners, not an evening cooking for a mechanic who was barely able to afford supermarket flowers. He thought about all the dozens of roses he'd purchased with nothing more in mind than impressing a woman. Dates had included the theater and dinner at an exquisite restaurant. He'd enjoyed himself for the moment, taken the woman home, and had rarely given her another thought.

Mara was different. She was the kind of woman who'd haunt a man if he walked away from her. Did her ex-husband feel that way now? Did he realize what he'd foolishly let slip away from him? Tough, Rick mused. You're the stupid one, buddy, not me.

Opening his apartment door, he saw her climbing the last few steps before the landing. While she carried Jessie in one arm, rumpled in her other hand was an envelope.

Briefly their eyes met, then her gaze shifted to the flowers. "You're not playing fair."

Rick noticed her smile was forced. "Why is that?"

"Now I'll owe you again. Those are beautiful. For me?"

"Jessie," he teased, hoping to see her smile deepen. It didn't. Instead her eyes brightened with tears. "What's happening here?" He transferred the flowers to the hand that clutched the wine bottle and caught the back of her neck.

"I'm being silly." She sniffed, but her eyes glazed with dampness. Mara closed them and fought the emotions tightening her chest. "This is a heck of way to start the evening," she murmured, trying for humor that she didn't feel. "Come on in," she urged and preceded him into the apartment. "Dinner will be ready—"

"Let me hold Jessie," he insisted and took Jessie from her. When he wrapped an arm around Jessie's bottom, she gurgled at him.

"She recognizes you now." Mara barely managed to say the words as her throat threatened to close.

"Go get a tissue," Rick ordered.

Though she gave him a quick, grateful smile, it didn't brighten her eyes. "I'm all right. Really." In his arm, Jessie squirmed and yawned. "And she's ready for bed."

As she took Jessie from him, Rick brushed a thumb across Mara's cheek. "If you need a shoulder, it's here whenever you want it." With the carefulness of touching something fragile, he framed her face with his hands and kissed her gently.

Something moved inside her. When she was at her weakest, he kept offering words of reassurance, a supporting arm, a sympathetic ear. "I'll remember that." The words came out haltingly. Sometimes she wanted so badly to lean on someone. "I might be a little while."

Mara stepped away before she went soft against him. "There's beer in the refrigerator." She glanced at the wine bottle he'd brought in. "Or if you want to open the wine, there are wineglasses in the cupboard above the silverware drawer."

Pride. Rick noted it in the firmness of her voice and the tilt of her head. "I'll be fine. Take care of her."

Mara nodded and headed for the bedroom. She could use a few minutes to herself. She felt like an absolute fool, but when she'd opened the envelope, a sense of failure had clawed at her.

She changed Jessie's diaper and held her for a long moment. Tenderly Mara traced a fingertip across her daughter's cheek. No matter what happened in her life, she had Jessie.

Rick uncorked the wine, poured two glasses and, carrying one of them, wandered to the window. He had no idea what was wrong, but he'd seen hurt, a deep penetrating kind of hurt, in her eyes. Amazingly, he'd become bound to this woman. Was it when he'd carried her into the hospital? He would admit now that it had been a special moment, one he'd never expected, one he'd never forget. How could a man ever erase from his memory the pain of labor crossing a woman's face or the happiness brightening her eyes at the same moment?

As the faint scent of Mara's fragrance drifted to him, he ended his unblinking stare at the roof of the brownstone next door. Facing her, he wondered if everything he felt for her now had begun to happen on that night. Who could ever pinpoint the exact moment when feelings for someone swept into a person's life? But for the first time in his life, he thought he might be falling in love.

"That didn't take long," Mara announced, spotting her car key on the kitchen table. "My car's fixed?"

Crossing to her, Rick snatched up the second wine glass. "It's fit to drive again."

Head bent, Mara dug in her purse for her key chain. "How—how much do I owe you?"

Rick knew avoidance when he saw it. Giving her time, he followed her lead and retrieved a folded paper from the pocket of his shirt. "Here's the bill."

One crisis after another, Mara mused. Feeling as if walls were tumbling in on her, she prepared herself and took the car repair bill from him. With her money tight, she hoped for the best. The amount surprised her. "It didn't cost very much."

Rick didn't tell her that she was only charged for the parts and not his time. "Bowman's Garage is reasonable."

"I'll remember that." The calmness in her own voice amazed her. "I'll get your money."

"Pay me tomorrow." He didn't buy her relaxed act. A hint of despair still glittered in her eyes. "Whatever happened is still upsetting you," he said, handing one of the fluted glasses to her.

He was right. The turmoil inside her lingered. Ever since she'd descended the stairs and taken the envelope from her mailbox, she'd been dealing with a myriad of emotions. The most intense was anger. Frustration came in a close second. Before her brave front failed her, she withdrew the crumpled envelope from her jeans pocket and offered it to him. "I received my divorce papers. It's official."

Mara gulped a hearty swallow of the wine, then wound a path around the sofa to the stove. "I don't feel badly for myself. What woman wants a man she can't trust?" Idly she moved the spoon through the Alfredo sauce that she had simmering on a low flame. "Steve had so many secrets. Secrets destroy trust. I'll never understand how someone can claim to love and tell lies. They make even the loving seem phony. Then you don't know what to believe, do you? That's what happened in my marriage."

Sidling close, Rick closed his hand over hers, stopping its movement. As she laid the wooden spoon against the side of the pot and faced him, he saw the hurt that had returned to her eyes. He was leading a life of deception, and the one thing she would expect from people around her was honesty. It was also the one thing he would never be able to give her. The bubbling of the sauce distracting him, with a sidelong glance he flicked off the stove burner. "He wasn't faithful?"

"Oh, much more than that. Yes, he would see other women." Strength came in spurts, Mara realized. As a wave of it crept forward, with determination she pretended concern with the sauce. Too much frustration and hurt threatened to erupt. Moving the pan to a cool burner, she waited a moment then leaned against the kitchen counter, needing its support. "He was out of town often, and he claimed he got lonely. That was supposed to explain everything—another set of friends, a whole different life." The glass again in her hand, she stared at the rose-colored liquid. "He even had a fiancée somewhere else." The arm Rick curled around her shoulder weakened her. A touch was all it took. Sagging against him, she spoke from her heart, sharing with him what she'd told no one. "It's Jessie I feel badly for. She deserves a father. And I failed her."

"You failed her?" Rick thought about the little one he'd held minutes ago and checked the fury bubbling within him but couldn't keep the incredulity out of his voice. "He's the one who bungled everything."

He didn't understand, Mara knew. The sense of failure and shame still shadowed her. Because she'd chosen poorly, her daughter was the loser.

"The man was a fool," Rick said softly. Linking his fingers with hers, he drew her away from the counter and back to the living room.

She released a quick, empty-sounding laugh. "My brother says good riddance."

Advice was easy to give when a person stood on the sidelines. "Has he ever been married?" Rick asked.

"No, he's a bachelor and loving it."

"Then he can't understand that you put a lot of yourself into something that's lost now. That hurts." In his own way, Rick identified with her. He'd struggled against odds to be the best reporter. He'd succeeded, won awards, then watched everything he'd worked so hard for slip from his grasp.

Mara studied him for a moment, surprised he comprehended exactly how she felt. "That's what I'm feeling. And foolish because of the choice I made."

"You couldn't have known he'd be like that."

"I blinded myself." The admission cost her. "I was so in love with him that I didn't want to see. But he couldn't have kept so much a secret if I hadn't let him. See? I'm responsible for what happened to me. It took a long time, but I finally realized that." She let out a hard breath. "And what hurt the most were the lies. How gullible I was. No one else is responsible for what happened in my life. Not Mama and Papa, not my sister or my brother or even Steve. I'm responsible."

"So he's exonerated?" Rick asked, growing angry with her.

"No, of course not."

"So why are you really upset?"

How did he read her so effortlessly? Mara wondered.

"It isn't because you picked a bastard or he played around." Rick believed the lies cut her deeply, but something else was gnawing at her. "What is it?" he persisted.

Tears slipped out. Mara wanted to squelch them and couldn't. "He doesn't want to see Jessie. He doesn't even care about her." On a sob, she blurted out, "She's his daughter, and he doesn't care."

At the raw pain clouding her eyes, Rick tentatively drew her closer. She deserved better than what the bastard had given her. He felt reluctance in her as if she were afraid he would let her lean on him again. He planned exactly that. "Come on. Use my shoulder."

Mara heaved a sigh and swayed against him, drawing strength and comfort from him.

"She won't lose a thing," he whispered against her ear.

Mara heaved a deep breath. Like a good friend, he'd paddled the way through muddy waters for her so she could see clearly. "You're thinking it might be better for Jessie to expect nothing from him than to have him drop in and out of Jessie's life, aren't you?"

"I'm thinking how smart you are." And special. She would shrug away bitterness and hurt. She would maintain those smiles and that optimistic outlook on life. She would do it all even if she ached inside, and she would do it because of her daughter.

Rick stroked her hair, trying to sort through conflicting thoughts of his own. He accepted that he could offer her nothing. If feelings deepened between them, he couldn't ask her to give up everything—her family and friends—to live a life on the run, to spend each day with uncertainty. In the end, he would do her more harm than good. But the rational thoughts refused to stick. During moments like this, with her close, with her heat against him, he wanted to believe in tomorrow, in a lot of tomorrows.

"I'm sorry." Mara kept her cheek pressed against his and wrapped an arm around his back. "I didn't mean to babble on about him." She felt his embrace tighten and knew that desire only edged the emotion making her cling. And what about him? Though he'd offered no insight into what bothered him, she sensed his needs, too, went beyond passion. Like two lost souls, they both yearned for closeness. "Will you celebrate with me?"

I'll give you anything you want. "The end?"

"Beginnings," Mara said softly against his jaw.

If he could be honest with her about anything, he could give her this much. "Mara, nothing's going to happen between us."

Rather than push her away, his words tugged her closer. "I know you're trying to be honest with me. I appreciate that. It's what I need most from the people around me. I value that more than anything."

"Tell me to leave," he appealed because he'd lost the willpower to let go this time.

How could she? she wondered. "I don't want you to."

"You deserve more," he murmured, then lightly kissed her.

It was his words that danced across her skin like a caress. "Don't stop," she whispered when his lips roamed to her cheek.

He didn't want to. Damn, he didn't want to. A flood of desperation storming him, he wanted to stretch every second with her. But while he ached to bring her pleasure, to give her a gentleness he'd only just discovered in himself, he knew he should pull away. He could offer her no future. But how could he resist what he'd been wanting for weeks? With her against him, her heartbeat pounding in rhythm with his, he made himself stare into her dark eyes to be sure she would understand as he spoke to her.

"You're going to say no promises, aren't you?" she whispered to make it easy for him.

He realized her straightforwardness, her frankness always made his deception, his guilt less burdensome. All he could give her was the honesty of his feelings. "I was going to say we shouldn't do this. I won't be good for you."

Even as he spoke, his thumb brushed her cheek with a tenderness Mara had caught fleeting glimpses of from the beginning. "I've been warned," she answered, turning her face to kiss his fingertips.

Desire darkening his eyes, he held her with a look. "You're not listening."

A sense of how right this was washed over her. She needed him. She wasn't sure of the future, but only now seemed to matter. "How can you be so sure you're right?"

He was sure of nothing. She was so giving, so accepting. He wanted to do the right thing. He wanted to pull away and walk to the door. And oh, God, he wanted her. He needed her brightness, her softness, her sensitivity in his life. And he swore softly, knowing he wouldn't walk away, couldn't stop now.

All caution fled from Mara with the caress of his mouth at the corner of her lips. She didn't want to think about tomorrows. The warmth of his breath fanning her face, she parted her lips, inviting and urging his tongue.

Nothing mattered but him. She heard the soft howl of the winter wind outside the windows, but if a blizzard raged, she didn't care. She drifted, becoming aware of the mouth teasing her, of the hands warming her body—of only this man. Intoxicated by the faint clean scent of soap on him, she slid her hands under the back of his shirt and skimmed naked strength, marveled at the muscles moving at her slightest touch.

With a slowness that rushed heat through her, he lightly tugged at the thin strap of her dress. The chill in the room whispered across her flesh when he unzipped her dress, when it fell to her feet. But she knew only warmth. Silk rustled beneath his fingers as he slid down her chemise, and the moonlight filtering in caught her nakedness. She felt no self-consciousness. She'd been yearning for him, aching for this moment. With trembling fingers, she sought the buttons on his shirt, then parted it. Briefly, she wondered if she would die with a need to be touched. To touch.

Then he drew her down to the carpet. She wanted to yield, to give him anything he wanted. Closing her eyes, she lost herself in him. Her skin tingled as he kissed her breast, caught a nipple. Heat stormed her with each stroke of his tongue.

As he tugged the last of the clothes from her, as he shifted to free himself of his own, she obeyed each subtle command of his hand. Though promises were left unsaid, she clung to him.

With each hot kiss on her breasts and stomach, she knew that nothing had been like this before. Breathless, she murmured his name. Her skin glowing, she urged him on.

Rick wondered if he would satisfy the craving for her. He tasted beyond his own desire, taking deeply, wanting to give her more. He'd never loved a woman. Several had caught his attention for a while. He'd been fond of them but had never felt love. Was this it? A madness to have more than seemed possible. A wild pleasure that wrapped around a person. A need for something as simple as the sound of her voice, a glimpse of her smile.

He teetered on an edge, sure that if he completely lost his balance, only she could save him. He took deeply of her mouth until she sighed, until he wanted to beg.

If he was to have only this night, it was more than he had ever allowed himself to believe possible. For with his every touch, every taste, he bound with her in a way he'd never conceived of.

On a raspy breath, she let her hand float over his hair, flutter at his bare shoulder, then urged him to meet the demand that would shred all link with reality. He rode on her pleasure, needing her to know what he could never say—that he craved more than a night of sultry heat with her.

She kissed him with a hunger that swept the breath from him. She stole control from him, returning pleasure as it had been received. A demand was in her caress, in the heat of her mouth enticing him, and a senselessness swept over him.

With heaving breaths, he caught her hips in his hands. His face inches above her, he searched her eyes. Dark and hooded with desire, they beckoned to him. Lowering himself to her, he knew he wasn't worthy of what she was offering. As her legs tightened on his back, as she opened herself to him, he sensed she was giving him her greatest gift. She was trusting him. After all she'd been through, she was still capable of finding the courage to give that to someone.

Flesh, damp and hot, blended. He reeled beneath the force of more than passion. Emotion tightened its grip on him as he drove harder, as she journeyed with him, as they blended as one. And he knew this would never be enough.

How much time had passed? Rick lay still, too content to move. For the first time in a year, he'd allowed himself to be distracted, to let a fog drift over his mind. He'd been aware of nothing outside the room or in it—except Mara. Feeling her arm draped across him, he kept his eyes closed for a moment longer. She snuggled, pressing her face into the curve of his neck. For so long, he'd been alone. He didn't have to be anymore. He had someone special in his life. Desperately, he wanted to play what-if games. What if he wasn't found this time? What if he could grab on to and keep hold of this life? What if he could make her a part of his world? So far, he'd been safe in Chicago. So far, he'd seen nothing suspicious. So far, he mused.

But there were no guarantees. "I'm sorry," he whispered.

To see him better, Mara raised her head. "For what? What we both wanted?"

Lightly, he grazed her bare hip with a finger. For everything I'll do that will hurt you, he mused.

Mara wished for a magician's skill, for a way to recapture the moments when he'd shared himself with her without reservation. But the mist of passion had lifted. He was already pulling back from her.

You deserve better. Rick pressed his lips to her temple. *Better than a quick affair with a man who might disappear one night as if he'd been nothing more than a figment of the imagination.* "You're more than I expected to find in my life." If he could promise her anything, he wished it was that he would never hurt her. "Sweet. You're so damn sweet."

Mara kissed him again, this time more deeply. A storm brewed inside him. She might never know why. But she believed what she'd felt with him had been real, that his emotions were honest. Pressing her lips against the curve of his neck, she stayed still, yearning for the closeness to continue. "I was looking for a description like sexy or seductive."

As she slanted her body across his, he strove for the lightness she seemed to want. "That's a given."

"Which one?" Mara feigned a narrow-eyed stare. "Careful how you answer. Sexy or seductive?"

It was crazy to believe this woman could be in his life forever. "Both."

"That's better." Tenderly, her lips skimmed his ear. "I think you are, too."

Suddenly he felt too lazy and content. "Do you need more convincing?"

Mara heard his hopeful tone. She sighed as he rolled her to her back. "A little more convincing would be all right. Then I'd be absolutely sure," she murmured and closed her eyes. Reasoning fled the instant he lowered his mouth to her breast.

Chapter Ten

Sleeping, he looked younger and vulnerable in the dawn's dim light. Feather light, Mara traced the sweep of his cheekbones and the strong line of his jaw.

Last night had been like the first time. She'd felt innocent. During those senseless moments, her body had glowed. She'd been alive with discovery, marveling at her own responses to his caresses, hungry with the power he'd given her.

Romance. She hadn't expected it in her life, especially so soon. When she'd been pregnant, she'd kept her spirits up thinking about the baby growing inside her, even though she'd been going through some of the most difficult days she'd known.

Deep within she'd been unsure if she would ever welcome another man in her life. Until Rick had entered it. When she'd least expected a man, when she'd needed someone, he'd been there for her.

And what did he feel? Was she imagining the way he looked at her? How could she be? When he held her, she felt loved. Bending over him, she kissed him gently. Though she was tempted to snuggle, she drew back and eased away, snatching her robe from a nearby chair.

The instant she'd left his side, Rick willed himself to open his eyes. On a lazy stretch, he folded an arm behind his head and drew in a deep breath. For a long moment, he lay quiet. He took in her lingering scent on the pillow beside him. There was more danger in the contentment he felt now than in all of the kisses and caresses they'd shared last night.

As the faint sound of Mara's humming drifted to him from another room, he roused himself from the bed. His clothes were draped over a chair in a corner of her bedroom. When had she retrieved them from the living room? When had they wandered from there to the bedroom? Last night his mind had been too filled with her to think about anything else.

He tugged on jeans, then padded into her kitchen. A bright white-and-yellow kimono-style wrap outlined her curves. Her hair looked tossed by the wind instead of his hands. As if she'd been up for hours, she flitted between the stove and the refrigerator.

Though he hadn't spoken, she must have sensed him. Over her shoulder, she presented a smile. "Good morning."

"Mornin'." Rick ran a hand over the bristles on his jaw. He had always dragged himself through the first few hours after awakening. "Is Jessie still sleeping?"

Not a great morning person, she assumed. On the other hand, she'd learned that motherhood didn't allow for leisurely wake-ups. "She won't be in another minute." With quickness, she scooped the white powdery formula out of a can and into the water of Jessie's bottle. "Coffee is made."

"I'm grateful," he mumbled. He meant to plop on a chair but found himself moving behind her. Unable to resist, he lightly grazed the curve of her hip.

It amazed her how easily his touch could make her quiver again.

"Are you acting or are you really one of those perky types in the morning?" he murmured against the side of her neck.

Mara breathed deeply. He was her lover. She was still trying to adjust to that. "Perky," she answered as she stroked the broad forearm draped across her belly. "What do you want for breakfast?"

He let his hand roam down her thigh. "Coffee will do."

"Not in this house," she chided lightly, nearly giggling as he nuzzled her neck and his beard tickled her.

"Were you brainwashed as a child to believe you...?"

"Can't start the day without breakfast," she finished and tilted her head back to see his face.

"But it's so early."

Smiling, Mara turned in his arms and kissed him. "We skipped dinner, remember?"

"Did we?" His answer came out slowly. At her movement, the V of her robe opened, and the swell of a breast caught his eye. He knew now her skin was softer than the pale yellow cloth covering it.

Mara released a self-conscious laugh. "Your mind is wandering, isn't it?"

His lips curved in a deep smile. "I'd be willing to skip breakfast, too."

"But Jessie wouldn't," Mara returned on a soft laugh. "So get your sea legs quickly," she mumbled when his mouth closed in on hers. I'm—" He caught the back of her neck, silencing her, and deepened the kiss.

"That helped," he murmured softly and meant it.

"I hope so. Laughter edging her voice, she caressed his jaw. "Because Jessie has her own unique way of waking up anyone."

Minutes later a smiling Jessie changed before his eyes. Rick swung a chair around, straddled it and watched her face redden a second before she bellowed. The cry went on while Mara settled on a stool at the counter and adjusted Jessie in the crook of her arm. Silence came as abruptly as it had started as Jessie's mouth closed around the nipple of the bottle.

Mara angled a look at Rick. Here was a beginning, she mused, realizing this was the first time she'd seen him relaxed, truly relaxed. Always he seemed on guard. She believed that, with time, whatever was troubling him would go away. "Since we're both off today, do you want to do something special?"

Being with her was special for him. But then only he knew how precious the moments were for them. He wondered how he could have believed that the fascination he had for her would disappear? If anything he wanted her more now. "What do you have in mind?"

She chose a lighthearted response. "We probably could fit some snuggling in."

As she'd hoped, he broke into a laugh. "Snuggling?"

"Yes, but we might want to go somewhere for a while. Someone in my family usually manages to drop in on my day off. By the time we get home, they'll be done trying to track me down."

With the ring of the phone, Mara maneuvered the bottle to her other hand. "Why is it that a solicitor inevitably calls when I'm feeding or changing Jessie?" she asked on a laugh before offering a hello.

The voice that answered her stunned her. She knew she paled, but she doubted she would ever be ready to hear Steve's voice again.

"How are you doing, Mara? I would have called sooner, but I've been busy. Out of town a lot."

Tensing, Mara coiled the telephone cord around a finger. "Your sister told me that you weren't around," she said flatly.

Steve spoke to her as if there hadn't been any abandonment or divorce. In the same light, offhand tone she'd heard dozens of times, he announced, "And I won't be. I'm only here for a few days."

She could visualize him slouched in a chair, a cocky grin curving his lips. It pleased her that she felt nothing for him, not even pain. "Are you aware of the bills you made?"

"Babe, I was trying to get restarted and didn't have a lot of money. I left you the money in the bank account. Remember?"

"All of three hundred dollars." The money meant nothing at the moment. Her stomach clenched as she waited for his request to see Jessie.

Instead, he said, "These demands for money, Mara, come at a bad time."

Too bad. Too damn bad. "I've had a few hard times, too." *Because of you.* "You know where I stand," she said tightly, wondering how he could totally erase his child from his mind. "Do you want to see her?" she asked because she didn't want him claiming later she'd never given him the opportunity.

"Who?"

Instant anger swept an urge over her to spiel off every despicable word she knew. "Jessie. The baby."

"You named her Jessie?"

Control cost her. She wanted to snap at him, but saw Rick studying her closely. "Didn't your sister tell you?"

"She said it was a girl."

Mara squeezed her eyes tight. He hadn't cared enough to ask more. "I don't have anything more to say to you." Furious now, she hung up the receiver. Her knees felt weak. Offering her back to Rick, she drew several deep breaths and looked down at Jessie. Could she feel her anger? she wondered as Jessie squirmed. "Are you still hungry?" Mara soothed in the softest tone she could muster.

Rick dropped to the stool beside her. "The ex?"

Tense, she sat with her back ramrod straight as if to move might break her. "Yes."

"Need to take a punch at something?"

Emotion tightened her chest. "The anger is gone," she answered with a quick shake of her head.

Rick didn't believe her. "Is it?"

She surrendered her attempt at a blasé look. "No, probably not."

What soft words would help? Rick wondered.

Mara offered the bottle to Jessie again. "I really thought I had control on this. But he never fails to do something more outlandish and rile me up again." She let out an impatient breath. "The other day, an old friend came into the restaurant and told me that he's engaged. This isn't the one he was engaged to while we were married. This is a new one. And she's pregnant." Despite her attempts to relax, tension bunched muscles in her shoulders. Every maternal instinct she possessed had risen within her to protect her baby. "Can you imagine? Not one child but two will have to call him their daddy."

Rick set a hand on her back and stroked lightly. "I doubt either one ever will."

The truth in his words couldn't be ignored. He was right, of course. A man who didn't want to see his child would always be a stranger. Jessie probably would never even know him. "So where do you want to go today?" she asked, longing to recapture the peace she'd felt before the phone call. "Do you like museums?" She sent him a quick smile and a silent message. *Help me forget.*

To alleviate the sadness shadowing her eyes, he followed her cue. "Ah, a cultural day. Will Jessie like that?"

With his question, Mara could have cried. He never forgot about Jessie. "She'll love the ride in her stroller."

"How do you know that?" Rick drained the coffee in his cup. "You couldn't have taken her out in it in the snow."

"I've been pushing her in the stroller around the apartment. She goes to sleep just like that," she assured him, snapping her fingers.

Rick caught her hand and kissed her knuckles. "You're crazy."

And you're wonderful. She outlined the deep smiling groove near a corner of his mouth. "Is that a yes?"

"It's a yes. I haven't seen much of the city since I arrived here."

Content with the day's plans, Mara leaned back and tilted her head up for a kiss. "Then let me be your tour guide."

Meaningfully, his eyes met hers. "You can be anything you want with me."

She wanted to ask, Do you mean forever? Aware that her own insecurities were intensifying, she struggled against them. She wouldn't spoil this and think about tomorrows. "I won't forget that later," she promised and winked back at him.

Children on class field trips and tourists ambled around the museum. Boots thumped across the entrance floor. Mara brushed flakes of snow from the top of Jessie's stroller while she scanned the huge lobby.

Rick looked up from the pamphlet of exhibits that had been handed to him at the door and noticed her visually circling the entrance. "What are you looking for?"

Unbuttoning her jacket, Mara scanned the lobby once more. "I thought there was a popcorn stand near here."

"You had breakfast," he said as a reminder of the bacon and eggs she'd cooked for them.

"It's almost lunchtime."

Amusement crept into his voice. "It's ten in the morning."

Mara pulled a face. "That's closer to lunchtime than breakfast."

A lazy grin hiked the corners of his lips. "Hunger makes you testy."

"It does not."

He held his hands up in a gesture of surrender. When she left for the rest room to change Jessie's diaper, he meandered to the information desk with a question about the popcorn stand. Weary of the lie he was living, he realized how much he longed to give her anything she wanted, including the truth about Van, about who he really was.

How? he wondered. He couldn't blurt it out. See-sawing thoughts shadowed him while he searched for the popcorn stand. He was still stymied when he re-traced his steps, popcorn in hand. As Mara strolled toward him, he struggled to banish troubled musings. "They moved the stand to another entrance."

Like a kid fixated on a candy counter, Mara eyed the popcorn. "Not very considerate of them," she murmured, dipping her hand into the bag. "It was nice of you to find this for me."

Rick raised his hands to her face, and with his thumbs he caressed her cheeks. He felt the onerous hand of guilt on his shoulder for not being honest with her. "You can have anything you want."

A pleasurable expression settled on her face. "Oh, you may be sorry you said that."

Three mouthfuls of popcorn later, she was rambling about the dinosaur exhibit.

For two hours he let her lead him through exhibits of classic cars and submarines. When she headed for the science exhibits about health and diseases, Rick balked, snagging her hand and forcing her to slow her quick stride. He plopped on the closest bench and tugged her down with him.

Mara dropped her head to his shoulder. "Tired?"

Amazed described what he was feeling. "How do you keep going?"

A tease sparkled in her eyes. "Okay, we'll forget the science exhibits." Mara swayed into him. "I love your smile."

"Is this called friendly persuasion?"

"Very friendly," she whispered against his mouth.

Laughter swelled up within him. Docilely he let her drag him through the dinosaur exhibit, and he ambled along a replica of a past century's Main Street, then traipsed with her through the aquarium and the Field Museum of Natural History. While they viewed the two-level, life-size Egyptian tomb, Jessie babbled nonstop at a mummy.

It occurred to Rick only later while driving toward the apartment building that he hadn't thought about Van all day.

As Jessie serenaded from the back seat, Mara hunted in the diaper bag for a bottle. "We're going to have to find someplace to stop so I can feed her," Mara announced when they sat in a traffic snag on the Michigan Avenue Bridge.

Nodding, Rick eased the car over the bridge and maneuvered it to the right lane, then negotiated a turn. "There's a restaurant at the end of the block. Do you want to feed her in there?" he asked, whipping the car into a parking garage.

"Here." Mara grimaced at Jessie's wail. "She has no patience when she's hungry."

"Takes after her mother."

A tease, she realized, opening her door to unsnap Jessie from her car seat. It seemed odd that she had so much to learn about him despite the intimacy shared. Because of talks about Steve, she knew now he was the kind of person who delved below the obvious. Most people liked to avoid what was uncomfortable for them. She doubted he'd ever shied from anything in his life, no matter how discomforted he might be. And she sensed he was a man who took nothing at face value. How much more was there to learn about him? she wondered. Did he have a dream, a goal as yet unfulfilled?

With Jessie snug in her arms and happily satiated with a bottle, Mara sent him another smile. "I bet you've never been on a date with a woman in an underground parking garage."

Rick draped an arm over the steering wheel and slanted a devilish grin at her. "Once. We steamed the car windows."

Mara rolled her eyes. "Why am I not surprised?"

"Seventeen and no class," he said self-deprecatingly, watching Jessie's little fingers curl around one of Mara's. "I was planning to take her to this snazzy restaurant after a dance, but we never got farther than the parking garage."

Mara bent Jessie forward to pat her on the back. "I'm having a hard time imagining you spiffed up in a tuxedo and standing at some girl's door, enduring her father's stare while you try to pin a corsage on her."

"No tuxedo. Nice blue suit. She didn't have a father. It was her grandfather. And no flowers. She didn't want them. She was too above all that kid's stuff."

"Oh." Mara arched an eyebrow. "One of those fast girls?"

"Best kind."

Mara stifled a giggle and spoke in a conspiratorial female-to-female way to her daughter. "Don't listen to him, Jessie."

Grinning, Rick enjoyed the view of mother and child. "What were you like?"

"Adorable," she returned lightly.

He easily believed that. "I have no doubt."

"Unlike the girl of your dreams, I wasn't above all that. I primped the whole day, even used phony nails."

"Was he worth it?"

"I thought so at the time. He was tall and skinny and the star forward on the school's basketball team. But he had no coordination on the dance floor. He stepped on my toes all night. One of the nails fell into the glass of punch he handed me. And I broke the heel on my shoes before the dance was over."

"It sounds as if it was a disaster date."

"I didn't think so."

Rick wasn't surprised. Repeatedly she'd shown that nothing got her down.

"He kissed me. My first kiss. That kiss made me forget everything else." The memory was a fond one for her. "And I saved my corsage between the pages of my diary."

"For how long?"

"Until my brother, the rat, read the diary to his buddies. I tossed the diary away then. It was the only choice I had since Mama said I couldn't get rid of Nick."

Rick heard affection in her voice. "You're close to him?"

"We're all close." A more serious look settled on her face. "Without them, I would never have made it through my pregnancy."

Rick found that difficult to believe. Despite her fragile appearance, she was tough.

"They were wonderful, though we had to restrain Nick, who nearly went after Steve."

"They know everything then about what your ex did?"

"I'd never keep a secret from them."

Rick merely nodded as he considered how close he'd been to telling her the truth about himself. He knew now that he couldn't.

By the time they returned to the apartment building, a sliver of a moon peeked out from behind swift-moving clouds.

Jessie slept through a diaper change. After tucking her in bed, Mara wandered to Rick in the kitchen. From the stereo drifted easy-listening music. To her surprise, he'd already started the coffee brewer. It hissed with the final drips. "It's been so long since I spent a day doing nothing but having fun."

On a stool by the kitchen counter, Rick took the toe of his one foot and pried off his unlaced work boot. "Getting blisters is fun?"

Because she noted a hint of a smile before he bent his head, his grumbling didn't faze her. Setting her elbows on the counter, she leaned toward him. "You should have worn more comfortable shoes."

Rick brought his face to hers. "You said *a* museum," he reminded her.

Mara gave in to a laugh. "Okay, next time we'll do what you want for the whole day."

As if sampling a taste, his lips nibbled at hers. "Snuggle," he murmured, using the word he'd teased her about saying earlier. "Or—"

"Or?" Feeling the fun in his mood, she eyed him warily as he rounded the counter to reach her. "Or what?"

"Or we could dance." His hand at her waist, he gathered her in his arms as if she belonged there.

"I thought your feet hurt," Mara baited, but saw no laughter in his eyes. Desire darkening them, they seduced her.

Slowly, he moved her with him, his thighs brushing hers. "For walking, not dancing."

The music floated around them while sensations hummed through her. In his arms, she swayed with him, against him. "What makes the difference?"

Caressingly his fingers trailed down her spine. "How close you are."

Warmth rushed through her. "Close is good." To taunt, she slid her hand over his thigh.

"Are you trying your feminine wiles on me?"

"It's later now." She felt his smile against her cheek. "I plan to have my way with you."

Rick caught his breath as delicate fingers fluttered back up toward his groin in a slow enticing manner.

"Is it working?" she murmured in his ear.

"It's working," he whispered, then captured her mouth beneath his.

Chapter Eleven

Hovering at the edge of wakefulness, Mara heard the clock on the bedside table ticking away minutes. She didn't move. Beside her in the bed, Rick burrowed deeper beneath a blanket and draped an arm across her waist.

Never in her wildest dreams had she felt such rightness with any man.

For the past four days, he'd romanced her. While flowers and nights of passion fulfilled womanly dreams, to Mara it was watching him amuse Jessie or hearing his voice soften with soothing words for her daughter that had tugged her heart with emotion.

Smiling now, she smoothed a hand over his backside. "Time to get up."

Rick mumbled something unintelligible but didn't budge.

She wasn't surprised. Slow at waking up, he snatched every minute he could before rising from the bed. After a final stretch, she shoved her pillow aside and forced her feet to the floor. While rounding the foot of the bed, she slipped on her robe. "Think breakfast," she urged softly, perching on the mattress beside him.

As he answered with a groan, Mara took a different course of action. She grazed his cheek with her knuckles. He remained dead to the world.

Leaning forward, she slipped a hand beneath the covers, and slowly she traced a path down the rock hardness of his stomach.

This time he stirred. "What time is it?" he murmured, his fingers shifting to the sharp angle of her hip.

Mara released a low husky laugh against his lips. "Too late for that."

"So you're teasing me."

Though he grinned as he spoke, humor wasn't the mood taking hold. Eyes deep with passion locked with hers. With a fingertip, she stroked a corner of his mouth. "I'm enticing you with what's to come later."

Arms tightening around her, he held her close. "Later is so far away."

Mara copied his frown, then broke into a smile. "Trust me. You'll survive."

Rick mirrored her expression. She had no idea how much he trusted her.

As he'd done every day, he left Mara's apartment before dawn, showered and dressed for work, then returned to share morning coffee with her. Mara kissed him goodbye, feeling like a wife with her husband.

The moment she closed the door, she hurried to slip on her parka. Her plan to step out the door went awry as she picked up Jessie and a strong odor drifted to her. Because of the extra diaper change, she was already five minutes late leaving for work.

One step outside, and Mara did an about-face to dress Jessie warmer. While a brilliant sun teased the mind to believe warmth fluttered on the breeze, a face-biting cold wind accompanied the daybreak brightness.

Because of the fifteen-minute delay in getting started, she got held up by a train at a light. Impatiently she tapped fingers on the steering wheel and counted cars. Fifty-five of them passed by. She sat through another red light, then got caught in a traffic jam a block from work. Running behind schedule always made her feel out of sync.

The feeling escalated the moment she opened the door of the restaurant. It bustled with customers, mostly workers from a nearby construction site.

A brief lull came around ten o'clock, but by noon the restaurant buzzed with the conversation of a lunchtime crowd.

Mara hustled to a table of five construction workers and took their order. She dealt with a growing impatience for her workday to end. In the middle of taking orders, she yearned for the quiet conversations she'd begun to share with Rick. She longed to see him, to watch the way he made a face for Jessie to stir her smile.

"Hey, Mara," a regular customer called out, breaking into her thoughts. "Does your papa know you're clock watching?" he teased.

Busing a table, she laughed and bantered back, "Don't be worrying about me. What are you doing, eating chili again, Joe?"

In his fifties and nursing an ulcer, Joe owned the television repair shop across the street. "I got new medicine from the doc. And a cast-iron stomach."

"Not for long if you keep eating like that." Mara gestured toward the hot red pepper in his hand. As he laughed, she hurried to the cook's counter to pick up an order.

"Mara, a phone call for you." Bianca offered the receiver while reaching for the plate Mara held. "I'll deliver it. Where is it going?"

"Table five. They have a pepperoni pizza, too." Mara stepped close and frowned with puzzlement. "Who is—"

Bianca sighed in the way an exasperated mother responded to her child. "Rick."

With twinges of pleasure rippling through her, Mara had no trouble ignoring her sister. Anyway, she was convinced that once her family really got to know Rick, they would like him better. With luck, that would happen on the night of her parents' anniversary party. "Hi," she said brightly.

"I know you're busy." She suspected he was smiling. "But I wanted to check with you. Do you want Chinese food tonight?"

"You're cooking?" she asked with surprise, bracing her backside against a counter so she could view the tables in her station.

Humor colored Rick's voice. "You jest. I meant that I'd pick it up. So you can have a day off. I owe you. You've cooked for me for the past four days."

"I didn't mind." She really hadn't. To her, cooking was like a hobby.

"So do you want that?"

"Great." He made her feel as if everything was wonderful in her life. She needed nothing more than what she had right now. Jessie and a man who made her believe again in the happiness that Steve had yanked out of her life without warning.

"And I'll get a video. The tenants' meeting can't last all night," he commented. "Oh, hell, I have to go. My manager is signaling me toward a truck. See you tonight."

"Okay, bye."

"Mara—"

She snapped the receiver back to her ear. "What?"

"I miss you."

She clung to his words for a long, breathless moment. Hard as she tried, she couldn't wipe an idiotic grin off her face even after she set the receiver back in its cradle.

Snowflakes flew at Rick's face when he stepped through the wide door of the stall at Bowman's Garage. Cold air stung his face and flapped at the bottom of his jacket as he dashed to his car. As he promised Mara, he whisked into the nearby Chinese restaurant, then the video store.

Five minutes later, hugging the huge bag of food, he plodded through a mound of soft deep snow to reach the steps of the apartment building. At the top one, his foot hit a patch of ice. Cursing, he lunged for the banister and clutched it.

"You need ice skates," a voice said behind him.

In a defensive crouch, Rick whipped around.

Carl Ingram cocked his head. "Easy."

That seemed impossible. Why would Carl come to see him tonight? Only trouble came to mind. "What are you doing out on such a lousy night?" Rick asked, straining to keep edginess at bay.

Carl shivered visibly and stuffed his hands into the pockets of his overcoat. "Let's go upstairs."

In silence, they climbed the steps. Rick waited only until they'd entered his apartment. "Okay, what's going on?" Unbuttoning his coat, Carl seemed to stall while Rick set the bag filled with food on the counter.

But Carl never wasted words. From the beginning, he'd been straight with Rick. "We want to move you."

Damn, no. Not now. "I don't want to move."

That brought up Carl's head. "Eric, it's a wise idea. You've been here a while. If you stay at this apartment too long, you could be found."

Rick shrugged out of his jacket. It took effort to stay calm. "You don't know that for sure."

"No, but it's my job to second-guess what's going to—" A quick, light knock on the door silenced Carl. His hand flew to the inside of his jacket and his shoulder holster.

"It's okay," Rick assured him.

Doubt narrowed Carl's eyes. "Are you sure?"

"I'm sure." Trust. Something he'd abandoned for a year had been found again because of Mara. He opened the door, and the darkness closing in on him seemed to fade.

Smiling, Mara leaned into him for a greeting kiss. "I'm starving."

In her arms, Jessie directed her toothless grin at him. No, he wasn't leaving this time. He couldn't.

Tipping her head back, Mara searched his eyes. He'd smiled; he'd kissed her back. But something was wrong. "What's the matter?" she asked. One step in, she saw the man leaning against a living room wall. In his early fifties with a receding hairline, he had a solemn look, but warm, friendly eyes. "Oh, I'm sorry. I didn't know you had company."

The curiosity in her expression assured Rick that he had no choice. "It's all right." He made the introduction, adding a lie that stuck in his throat. "Carl's my cousin."

Mara saw no family resemblance at all, but Rick had mentioned a cousin, had said they saw each other only once in a while, and Carl traveled a lot. She shifted Jessie to her other arm. To finally meet someone Rick knew opened another door for her. She would have liked to quiz Carl. Did he know Rick as a child? Or was it only after the years in foster homes that Rick had found a relative? What had he been like? How special are you to him? "Rick told me you travel often. What do you do in your job?"

As Carl's gaze never wavered from her, she had the distinct impression of a man used to studying others. "I handle security for special individuals."

She immediately thought of the movie *Bodyguard*. "Like celebrities?"

"Sometimes." He flashed what Mara interpreted as a polite smile before he began rebuttoning his overcoat. "I should go, Rick. The weather is bad. It'll probably take me all night to get home."

"I can't help you if you get stranded somewhere." Rick sidestepped Mara to open the door for Carl. "I'll probably be stuck here, too."

Carl's gaze met his with understanding. "No better place to be than home."

"That's right." Rick wondered at what point this private, silent communication with Carl had begun to exist. He didn't know, but was grateful for it. Carl knew now the risks he'd take for any moments he could have with one woman.

Spreading a blanket on the rug for Jessie, Mara studied both men. No real affection existed between them. Why not? In her family, relatives hugged or placed a hand on a shoulder. Even when not touching, camaraderie dominated every gathering. She saw none of that between Rick and Carl. Perhaps mutual respect but nothing else. "Maybe Rick could call you, and you could find time to come to dinner some night," she suggested as she placed Jessie down among a few toys.

"I'd like that," Carl answered friendly enough, but a network of frown lines wrinkled his forehead.

Mara tucked away a little flutter of nerves when Rick stepped into the hallway with Carl and closed the door. With time alone, she circled Rick's apartment. It was the first time she'd been inside. It struck her immediately that the rooms revealed nothing of the man who lived there.

She collected sentimental knickknacks. She had a stuffed panda her brother had won at a church bazaar and given to her when he was sixteen, and a glass paperweight of a miniature White House that she'd bought during her class trip to Washington, D.C., and a crystal rocking chair she'd spent too much for when she'd been pregnant. Bits and pieces of her whole life adorned the rooms in her apartment.

His contained nothing. The only sign of who he was were the books on an end table. He liked to read. More evidence of that existed in the stacks of newspapers, issues from New York and Miami. And on the table, one of them was folded to a crossword puzzle. Had she not known him, had she merely wandered into the room of a stranger, she'd have pegged him as an intellect.

"Did you check out dinner yet?" Rick asked, closing the door behind him and staring at her slender back.

Mara whirled around. Too many questions suddenly threatened the joy she'd found with him. "If Carl's family, why don't you talk about him more, see him more?"

Pleasurably he fingered a strand of her silky hair before he strolled to the bag of food. "We're distant, Mara."

Mara puzzled over his answer. Raised in a family where cousins remained as close as siblings, she couldn't relate to such emotional distance. As Jessie tossed her fuzzy plush lamb aside and her eyebrows veed with a frown, Mara lifted her into her arms. "He doesn't have a wife or children?" Mara asked and joined him at the kitchen counter.

Rick withdrew white cartons from the bag. "No." No amount of excuses eased the guilt bearing down on him from the lies. "He's too busy with his job." That much was true, but the rest of the deception gnawed at Rick.

"That's a shame." Beside him now, Mara caught a whiff of something enticing and handed Jessie to Rick. "What did you get for dinner?" She peeked into a white carton. "Oh, you got cashew chicken. I love it. And—" She peered into another carton.

"Beef and broccoli? I like that." Rick laid his head against Jessie's. Damn, this was all wrong. He'd never thought before about the necessary lies to others that had rolled off his tongue. But she wasn't anyone. She was the woman he loved.

Love. The emotion slammed at him. He'd found the woman he yearned to share a lifetime with, and he should get the hell out of her life now.

"Where are the plates?" Mara repeated, inclining her head to place herself in his vision.

Rick snapped himself back from what he could only view as a fantasy. "I'll get them."

While exchanging Jessie from his arms to Mara's, his forearm brushed her breast. A tiny tremor shot through her. She was amazed. Despite nights of loving, even the simplest, most casual touch brewed sensations. Mara set Jessie on the blanket. The moment she was placed on her back, she rolled from it to her side. "For days she's been working hard at rolling over," she said on a laugh. "It's remarkable. It seems as if it were yesterday when she was born, and now she's trying to roll over. Soon she'll be scooting around, then walking and—"

As she stopped midsentence, Rick pivoted with the plates in his hands to see what had distracted her. She stood beside the small, scarred desk in a corner of the room and stared at the computer and the stack of manuscript pages. Rick cursed himself. He'd meant to put it all away before she came, but with Carl's arrival, he'd gotten sidetracked. Mara fingered one sheet of paper. "What is this?"

Make light of it, Rick told himself. "What can I say? I'm a frustrated writer." In a way, that was true. He'd had trouble giving up his past. Since he'd walked away from his job at the newspaper, he'd needed to write.

The puzzlement knitting her forehead lifted. Pleasure swept across her face. "I've never known a writer before. What do you write?"

That she was impressed would have pleased him a year ago. He'd have liked to share this with her. But this was all he had left of his other life. It was also the one link to Eric Lassiter. "I'm not done," he answered, crossing to her. He stacked the papers before she could read any of them.

Mara straightened her back. With one simple gesture, he'd slammed the door barely opened to her.

Uneasiness slithered through her. He'd made love with her. Why hadn't he mentioned this to her?

"It's nothing."

Mara caught the coolness, knew he was distancing himself, and she couldn't do anything about it. To veil emotions, she strolled to the counter and the bag of food. "I guess we should eat."

Rick didn't need to see her face. Disappointment, no, it was hurt that edged her voice. He cursed himself for overreacting. The manuscript didn't have to link Rick Sloan to Eric Lassiter. Why would it? Indecisively, he held the papers, aware how easily he might lose more than the secret that he wrote. Excuses, like lies, came easier with experience. He drummed up a quick one. "I acted dumb about this, Mara. Insecurity," he said on a laugh. "I wasn't prepared for anyone to read it yet."

That made sense to her. When she was younger, she'd made a patchwork quilt for her mother for Christmas. She'd been protective of her work, not wanting anyone to see it until she'd finished. "I'm sorry. I shouldn't have—"

"You caught me by surprise. When it's done, I'd like you to read it."

Instantly, her face lit up. "Thank you. I'd like to. What is it about?"

He'd written about what he knew. "A reporter caught up in a story about a pillar of society involved with drugs."

Mara scooped spoons of rice onto her plate. "Had you done any writing before this?"

Sidling close, Rick handed her another carton. He could give her a little. "I worked on a newspaper for a while."

Her spoon stilled in midair. "Then why aren't you now? Why are you a mechanic?"

Rick shrugged. "I couldn't keep the job." That sure as hell wasn't a lie. Circumstances had forced him to give it up. "And the everyday hassles of the job got to me." Like trying to stay alive. He couldn't forget the months of living hell when he'd risked his life to gather evidence for a conviction.

Because he needed the closeness with her, he stepped up behind her and slipped his arms around her.

Mara laid her head back on his shoulder. "I think this is wonderful, Rick. So many people claim they're writers and have never finished writing anything. You have a beginning, middle and an end."

She liked everything neatly tied up, he reminded himself. She liked certainties, and he could offer none.

As he splayed his fingers over her belly, she turned in his arms to look up at him. "We're never going to get to that tenants' meeting this way."

He wanted more time to hold her close before—before he had to let her go forever. Overwhelmed by the need, he kept a tight embrace on her and kissed the bridge of her nose. "Couldn't we forget about it?"

In a slow, enticing manner, he traced his tongue along her earlobe. He could easily persuade her to do anything. Mara giggled at the play of his mouth. "Got to go."

He heard a sigh and pressed his forehead to hers. "I'm not staying more than an hour," he grumbled.

* * *

The meeting lasted two hours. The Valquez family, this month's hosts, stuffed them with homemade tamales, miniature enchiladas and salsa and chips.

To the sound of Mr. Weisman arguing with Mrs. Osgood about his leaky faucet being a more important complaint than her broken window, Mara preceded Rick into the hallway. "Spokesman," she murmured, shaking her head while she cradled a sleeping Jessie. "Why did they choose me to be their spokesman with the management company?"

His eyes danced. "Must be because of your persuasive way."

"Or because I'm too soft to say no to anyone," she returned self-deprecatingly.

"Mara." Mr. Weisman scurried from the Valquez's apartment to reach them. "Mara, you have to come back in. We need to add a few more things to our list of complaints."

Mara wondered how to refuse. Blame her parents, she mused. They'd taught responsibility to commitment to all their children at early ages. "I really have to get Jessie in bed, Mr. Weisman."

Always helpful, Mr. Weisman turned a questioning look up at Rick. "Couldn't you put her to bed?"

Rick stared dumbfoundedly at him. How had he dodged neighbors' urgings that he go with Mara when she presented their demands to the management company only to find himself now being volunteered for baby-sitting? "You want *me* to baby-sit?"

Mara repressed a smile at his bewildered look. She'd seen him with Jessie—gentle and patient and loving. "She likes you," Mara offered as an assurance.

"Couldn't you?" Mr. Weisman repeated.

Rick gauged the situation. Jessie was sleeping soundly in Mara's arms. How much trouble could occur if she was sleeping? "Okay, I'll meet you at your apartment."

"She'll probably sleep until I get there." Mara transferred her to his arms, then kissed his cheek. "Thank you." She obeyed Mr. Weisman's urging hand on her elbow and turned to enter the Valquez's apartment. "Oh." She balked at the doorway, swinging a look back at Rick. "If she turns onto her tummy, she gets mad because she doesn't know how to get onto her back again. And if you have to give her a bottle, don't forget to burp her."

"Burp?" Nodding, Rick climbed the steps to Mara's apartment. He could do this. If she kept sleeping, this impromptu baby-sitting job would be a cinch.

He learned that was a big if.

He'd barely taken off his shoes and flicked on the television. Within five minutes of dropping to the sofa to enjoy a basketball game, Jessie stirred.

She whimpered only once in the playpen.

Rick shot across the room to her. Though her eyes remained shut, she gnawed on a tiny fist. On a deep breath, he wondered how someone so small could make him feel so inept.

Rick scanned the playpen for the pacifier, just in case. No warning came. A wail suddenly pierced the quietness. Red-faced now, her legs kicking, she screamed nonstop.

"Ssh," Rick soothed, leaning over her. "It'll only be a minute. I promise." He gave her the assurance while charging to the counter for the bottle.

Her wail intensified.

Rick sprinted back to the playpen. As if starving, she was sucking on her fingers. "Just so you know. This is a first for me," he said, lifting her. Somehow he wedged the nipple of the bottle past her hand and into her mouth.

As quiet reigned, he settled on the closest chair with her in his arms, feeling a touch smug. While her mouth tugged at the nipple, a tiny hand curled around one of Rick's fingers. He couldn't resist stroking her soft, downy hair. "You have to be a good girl right now. Your mommy has a problem."

She let the nipple slip out of her mouth, then gurgled a few sounds as if answering him. Her little mouth moved more. At first no sound came out, then something that resembled the word *oh* flowed from her throat.

Rick laughed. "Are you going to talk as much as your mommy does? I can hardly wait." But would he ever hear Jessie say a coherent word or watch her attempts at crawling or see her walk?

Rick pressed his mouth to Jessie's forehead. How had this happened? he wondered. How had this little girl become so important that he physically hurt at the thought of leaving her one day, at never witnessing the small triumphs in her life?

"I'd like to tell you I'm here to stay," he said softly when she fixed a stare on his face, as if memorizing it. "That you can depend on me. That I'll be here to catch you when you start walking. That I'll help you when you're learning to ride a bike. But I probably won't be, Jessie."

Rick kept the nipple close to her mouth until she resumed sucking enthusiastically. "I'm sorry, Jessie. You don't know how sorry I am." As raw emotion swelled up in his chest, on a long breath he laid his head back on the cushion of the sofa and closed his eyes. *Be a part of my life.* He didn't bother to say the words she wouldn't understand. But he wanted this child and her mother. At some moment, he had let down his defenses and two females had rushed in. His heart welcomed them even as his mind resisted.

He wanted more than he had a right to—a part of their world. Nestling Jessie closer, he drew a hard breath. Hell, he wanted it all.

Mara had thought she would never escape. Quietly, she opened her apartment door. With a quick scan of the room, she was surprised not to see Rick anywhere. Ever since she'd left him, she'd wondered how he was surviving one of the ultimate tests of friendship, taking care of someone else's child.

An announcer on the television droned on statistics about someone with Michael Jordan potential. Mara closed the door and walked softly across the room to flick off the television. Then she saw Rick, sprawled on the sofa and sleeping. His soft snores blended with Jessie's as she lay on his chest, her eyes closed.

Squatting beside the sofa, Mara ran a hand lovingly over Jessie's head, then reached up and outlined Rick's mouth. His eyelashes flickered before he opened his eyes. In them, she thought she saw what she longed for—love. "You snore," she teased, smiling.

"That was Jessie."

"Oh." She bent forward and pressed her mouth to his. "Thank you."

He plunged a hand into her hair to keep her face close and let the strands twist around his fingers. He knew the softness beneath her strength, the sensuality beneath her sweetness. "My pleasure," he whispered. This time, he took her mouth deeply.

Mara felt the edge of passion, the hint of urgency. "I'll put her to bed."

It amazed him that every fantasy he'd had about her had come alive. "Mara."

At the huskiness in his voice, she stilled in taking Jessie from him. "What?"

"Your ex is a fool." With care, he ran a callused finger over Jessie's cheek.

If she hadn't loved him before, Mara would have now. Carrying Jessie to her crib, she savored his words, wrapping herself in the feeling that had made him say that. He loved her daughter as if she were his own. She felt almost drunk with the joy of that realization. Blinking back tears, she kissed Jessie goodnight, then laid a blanket over her.

Rick lounged against the doorway and drew a hard breath, moved by the scene before him. A frantic urge swept over him to cling to this moment of her putting her daughter in her crib. In the dim light of the room, he felt the bright warmth of sunshine as if the shadows chasing him even in daytime had disappeared. He knew he was more vulnerable now than he'd been since Frank Van's first threat against him.

"She's sleeping." Mara stepped into his embrace. "I love you," she whispered.

For a long moment, he held her, letting her words drift over him—caress him with their meaning.

Because her heart had soared with the emotion, she'd needed to tell him. Now with his silence, she had doubts. Why had she foolishly blurted that out? "I'm not expecting anything," she assured him. She ran her hands down his chest, her fingers working at the buttons of his shirt. "I know you don't want to give it, but I needed to tell you."

Rick wanted to say the words back, to tell her that she and Jessie were all he wanted in the world. He said nothing. An arm at her waist, he tugged her closer until her soft contours blended as one with him. Slowly, he backed up, leading her toward the other bedroom, deepening the kiss to tell her what he felt in the only way he could.

Mara melted against him. There was a desperateness in his kiss, but the hands raising her T-shirt moved with tenderness before tossing it aside. The gentleness went on. He skimmed fingertips across her flesh. If there was a chill in the air, she wasn't aware. With her breasts flattened against his chest, with her mouth clinging to his again, nothing mattered but the raw, yearning building within her.

As she strained against him, they tumbled onto the bed. Mouths clung in a kiss that was hard, a kiss meant to link them. Frantic movements controlled them until flesh touched flesh. A headiness, a hunger swept over her. As he hurried her now, she rushed him. She tasted and taunted. Every breath drawn, every sigh, every beat of her heart was for him. Love bound her to him. Love made her ache to give. Love overwhelmed her.

She moaned as he touched the sharp point of her hip, the silky softness of her thighs, and found the warmth between them. A fingertip grazed her with a slow, tantalizing stroke. Mara stopped breathing. Had she ever yearned so much? Had she ever longed like this, trembled from it?

Beneath her hands, his muscles rippled. As his mouth roamed over her, she felt the rough stubble on his cheek. Even it sprang her to life with sensation. Shifting, she taunted herself and rained kisses over him, memorizing every inch of his lean body that she could reach. Muscles quivered beneath her touch. He murmured something soft, something unintelligible. Words didn't matter. She wanted to give, to please him. Her pulse pounding, she pressed her mouth against his chest, then inched lower. Every rational thought was gone. All that mattered was hot, damp flesh. When he traced his tongue over sensitive skin, she sought him.

A storm raged. Rick sucked in breaths. Before, she'd only consumed his thoughts. Now she possessed his soul. She fed his excitement. He'd never known it could be like this, but then, he'd never loved before.

He needed another minute. One more minute. But a lover's pace succumbed as she flirted with his control. With a swiftness that rocked him, she seduced until a wildness to have her swept over him.

Whispering her name, he slipped into her. "I love you, too."

The words torn from him echoed in her mind. He loved her. He'd said the words. That was all that mattered. He really loved her. Mara clung, melting against him. Then his mouth was on hers. Pleasure and torture blended.

She moaned his name, but needed to see his eyes, watch his face. Framing it with her hands, she arched and drew him deeper and filled herself with him.

Had she imagined what he'd said? Would he regret saying those words now? she wondered. Breathless, she grazed his warm, damp back and clung to keep him near a moment longer. "Would you say that again?"

"I'll say it forever," he murmured against her cheek, but he wasn't sure she would always hear him. "I love you."

The words made her senseless. "It's all that I'd hoped for. Do you know that?"

"I know there's never been anyone like you in my life," he said fiercely. In a possessive move, he stroked her hip with his fingers. "I know I've never loved before."

His words stilled her heart. Lifting her head, she stared at him. In fascination, she watched the smile form in his eyes before his lips curved. "Never?" She curled against him so the full length of his naked body was against hers.

"Never," he whispered, longing to believe they could have forever.

Chapter Twelve

Morning sunlight poured over the bathroom floor. Water rushing down on them in the tight confines of the shower, Rick kissed her sudsy shoulder. "You soap hog." Steam fogged the air, but he saw all he needed to. He doubted she'd ever looked more beautiful.

Mara lifted her face to the wetness before she wiggled around in his arms. He'd stunned her with a passion that had seemed almost desperate the night before. "You said we had to take a shower together."

While her soapy hand roamed down his chest, he spread light kisses over her face, flushed and gleaming from the heat. "Because Jessie is an early riser," he reminded her.

On a laugh, Mara tossed back her wet hair. They'd already played audience to Jessie's early-morning activity. Since then, she'd gone back to sleep. "What do you want for breakfast?"

Lightly, he nibbled at the side of her neck and caressed skin slick with dampness, letting his fingers roam down her hip and over her buttock.

Another laugh rushed from her throat. "Not too subtle," she managed to say on a quick breath as his fingers slipped between her thighs. Closing her eyes, she doubted she'd ever been quite so happy.

"You'll come tonight?" she'd asked him about her parents' anniversary party before they'd separated to head for work.

Denying her anything had become impossible. Rick had said yes, but the thought of spending an evening with the Vincetti clan to celebrate her parents' anniversary worried him.

They weren't happy she was seeing him. Some sixth sense in several of them had kicked in about him. It went beyond her older sister's wariness or her parents' worry. The brother smelled trouble for his sister.

No, it wouldn't be a relaxing night. But because Mara wanted him to be there, he would go.

"I'm leaving early today," Wes declared, clanging a wrench as he retrieved it from his toolbox.

"You're really getting married?" Rick asked, not for the first time. Earlier, when Wes had announced his plans, Rick had responded with disbelief.

Wes grinned like a Cheshire cat. "Guess there's a right one for all of us," he answered. As if oblivious to everything around him, he withdrew a pocket-size notebook from his shirt pocket and flipped several pages. "Got lots to do. Go home, clean up, make dinner reservations, get flowers for Michelle and the others, pick up her parents from the airport."

Rick smiled at the excitement in Wes's speech. Women had no idea of the power they wielded. Rick considered how easily and effortlessly Mara had talked him into something. Because of her, he'd gone to a tenants' meeting and spent a day at museums. Because of her, he was willingly going to do the unthinkable and surround himself with strangers tonight at her parents' anniversary party.

Beside him, Wes muttered, "I'll never get everything done. We should have waited until next week."

"So why didn't you?"

Wes looked sheepish with an admittance. "I wanted to marry her now."

"Before she changed her mind?" Rick jibed.

Wes tucked the notebook back into his pocket and, aware of the manager's eagle eye on him, pretended deep concentration under the hood of a truck. "Very funny."

As Wes gave a nervous glance in the direction of the wall clock in the manager's office, Rick took pity on him. "Okay, what do you want me to do?"

Wes matched his grin. "You'll help?"

"I'm best man."

Zealously Wes slapped him on the back. "Knew I could count on you."

Rick wished that were true, but beyond the next hour or two, no one could rely on him for anything.

Wes chuckled. "You think I'm crazy, don't you?"

Rick could have told him that he understood the longing to be with a certain woman.

"I don't care if I sound like an idiot." Gripping the wrench again, he studied the truck's engine. "You'll see. Someday you'll meet the right one."

Not someday. He'd already met her.

Mara scurried in high gear around the restaurant. Though she and Bianca had tried to convince their parents to take the day off, a special treat for their anniversary, Papa adamantly refused. Her mother had put in a half day, then left for the hairdresser. Mara finished her side work, filling catsup bottles and checking sugar and salt and pepper containers. With Bianca's assurance that she would deal with any after-lunch customers, Mara left.

Errands took up most of her afternoon. Fortunately Mrs. Torrence volunteered to baby-sit Jessie for a few hours. After carting in groceries and the anniversary cake, Mara scooted the vacuum cleaner around her apartment, set up the urn of coffee, then took a shower. While she was in the middle of dressing, Rick called. She ignored the quick tug of disappointment his words stirred as he explained about Wes.

"They're getting married before five," Rick told her. "Wes invited the witnesses, me included, and his parents to dinner. I'll be a little late."

Giving herself a pep talk, Mara dressed. He wouldn't let her down tonight. He knew how much she wanted him at the party.

By seven that evening, her apartment bulged with the Vincetti clan, friends and neighbors. Rooms echoed with the buzz of conversation as everyone talked at once.

"So where is he?" Nick asked, eyeing the cake Mara had set on the table.

She wondered the same thing but veiled her own doubts. "Don't be so impatient. He'll be here. A friend at work was getting married. He called and told me that he'd be a little late. He went to the courthouse with them to be a witness."

Skepticism entered her brother's voice. "The courthouse closed hours ago."

Mara cast an exasperated look at him and slapped his hand before he could take a swipe at the frosting with his finger. "He couldn't go and not share in some of the celebration afterward. Anyway, he's not the only one missing. Aunt Clara isn't here yet, either."

While she arranged forks and napkins for guests to pick up easily, he continued to hover. Mara expected more questions.

Her brother proved as predictable as ever. "What have you learned about him?"

If she dodged him, he would hound her. "I know he worked at a newspaper for a while."

"That doesn't make sense." Nick palmed a handful of nuts from a glass bowl. "If he did, why would he be working as mechanic. What newspaper?" he asked between chews.

"I didn't ask."

Disbelief darkened his face. "Why not?

He studied her for so long that Mara nearly squirmed. "Why should I have?"

Nick met her defiant look with a challenging one. "So I could check him out."

"I don't want you to. He's a good man."

A hint of irritation edged his voice. "Don't be fooled."

As if someone had thrown a punch at her chin, she raised it. "That's not what you mean. Don't 'be a fool' is what you really mean, isn't it?" she asked, leveling a steady stare at him.

"Hey, don't get in a temper."

More than angry, she was scared that he would slip doubts into her mind. "Stop asking questions."

Nick closed a hand over hers, halting her from re-arranging napkins. "Why are you so defensive?"

Because he's touched me. Because I've felt the gentleness of his caress, the heat of his body. "Because I trust him."

"It's that simple?"

"Yes, that simple," Mara returned. He'd told her that he loved her. She believed in him. "And don't start talking like Bianca about him being a felon. I know him. He's not a criminal."

"That's probably true."

Mara whipped a look up at him. "You checked on him?"

"I did it because I love you."

Even understanding the emotion that had motivated him to snoop into Rick's life, she wanted to punch her brother.

"He has no background, Mara," Nick said simply.

Mara felt a thread of genuine amusement taking over. "You mean he doesn't have a rap sheet—"

"There's nothing on him," Nick cut in. "There's no driving violations, no jury duty, no service record. He doesn't seem to have existed until months ago."

Her brother's voice was like a distant echo. Confused, she took a moment to let his words register. But none of what he'd said made sense to her. "That's impossible." Too many thoughts mingling in her mind, she shook her head, rejecting any that fueled doubts. "I don't know why you couldn't learn anything. But sometimes what a person feels is more important than anything else. Nick, he's important to me."

A deeper frown etched a line between his eyebrows. "How important?"

"Important," she said to make him understand. "Get to know him tonight. You'll like him." She inclined her head, forcing his gaze to meet hers. He didn't look happy. "Please, try. Please."

"Oh, hell." More tenseness etched his features. "You're sure?"

"I'm sure," she said without hesitation.

The moment Rick left the restaurant and the happy couple, he sprinted across the street to his car. Cold night air hit him in the face. On a muttered oath, he shivered, but not from the chill in the air. Hair on the back of his neck rose.

After months of looking over his shoulder, gut instinct made him scan his surroundings. He knew instantly. Someone was watching him.

Clamping a hand over the top of his car door, he peered at the dark buildings across the street. As a shadow moved, he dived inside his car. He grappled for common sense to stay calm, even as his heart thudded with panic. Crouched down in the dark interior of the car, he fumbled to slip the key into the ignition. Before he flicked it on and the engine revved, a strategy formed in his mind.

After three tire-screeching turns and backtracking a block, he lost the guy in the dark green sedan. Adrenaline still pumping, he braked outside a convenience store. Several moments passed while he checked cars driving by. Feeling safer, on a run, he hit the nearby telephone booth. Not once had he bothered Carl at home—until now. "I'm being tailed," he said instead of a greeting to Carl. "The guy's in a dark green sedan."

"Damn. You spotted him?" He heard Carl's heavy sigh. "Sorry we alarmed you. He's our man."

"What?" Rick slumped against the wall of the telephone booth and ended his scrutiny of every car that passed by.

"My department felt you needed extra protection since you weren't willing to leave. We put someone in the building next to yours, too."

"Call him off," Rick demanded.

"Eric—"

"Call him off." He was tired of it all, he realized. He wanted to live like other people. He wanted to love, to plan a future.

Minutes later he climbed the apartment building stairs to the sounds of merriment. At the fourth floor, someone unfamiliar to Rick swung open and held Mara's apartment door. Slim and dark haired, he greeted Rick with the same kind of friendliness Mara revealed. "I'm a cousin. Joey."

Rick answered in kind. "A neighbor. Rick."

"Glad to meet you. Go in. I'm headed for more ice," he said, already steps away.

Noise and laughter dueled with the sound of *La Bohème* coming from Mara's stereo. Voices were raised in glee. Children chased around. Laughter mingled with good-natured arguments, and the aroma of spices and tomato sauce permeated the air.

Lingering at the door, Rick jammed his hands into his pockets. He felt like a man who'd just stepped on foreign land.

A frail, gray-haired woman wearing a black shawl pointed a thin finger at a man a head taller than her.

Nearby, a young woman with flashing dark eyes stood with hands on hips. "Don't be looking at her like that again, Carmen," she was scolding the curly-haired, muscular man beside her.

He grabbed her hands and kissed her knuckles. "Stella, Stella, I love only you."

With a sweeping glance, Rick spotted Mara setting plates on her kitchen table. In the middle of it rested a long cake covered with white frosting. An intense longing flooded him for something as simple and re-assuring as a smile from her. Rick shut the door behind him and took a step forward, only one.

A man with kinky white hair and a deeply lined face pumped his hand. "You're a friend of...?"

"Mara's. I'm Rick."

"Good to meet you. I'm her Uncle Luigi."

More polite introductions followed. Rick doubted he would remember all the names. He nodded agreeably to several comments tossed at him.

"Mara's baby is beautiful."

"She's a good daughter, so pretty, so smart."

Then a whiskey-sounding voice intruded. It belonged to a short, rotund woman. "Who's this?" She muscled her way to him. "I don't know you." Her dark eyes pinned Rick, then darted to Mara's father, Vito. "I don't know him."

Vito laughed. "My sister has to know everyone," Mara's father explained before making the introduction. "This is Mara's Aunt Gina."

Gina's broad face widened with her smile. "It's good. Mara has a boyfriend. Always love is in the air." Her chubby hand curled over Vito's. "I was so happy when you married Teresa. So in love, they were," she said to anyone who would listen.

"Still am," Mara's father returned and curled an arm around his wife's shoulder as Teresa sidled close.

Gina's attention switched back to Rick. "You, eat. You can't live on love alone. The food is in the kitchen."

Sneaking up behind Rick, Mara felt a warm glow kindling within her at seeing him in the midst of a family gathering. "Aunt Gina can overwhelm," she murmured in his ear and slid an arm around his waist.

The yearning to touch overwhelmed Rick. Shifting his stance, he caught strands of her hair. "It's a Vincetti trait?"

"Did I overwhelm you?" she asked softly with an impish sparkle in her eyes.

"Constantly," he assured her.

Mara took his hand and urged him to follow her. "Come with me. I'll find you a beer."

As Rick fell in step beside her, Mara's brother-in-law blocked their path to the kitchen. "It's late to tell you this." In an affectionate gesture, Angelo set a hand on Mara's back. "But thanks for taking care of Mara the night she had Jessie."

Rick hadn't expected this. He'd been prepared for questions from her family, not words of gratitude. "It was no problem."

Mara smiled up at him. He might not remember how annoyed he'd looked that night, but she did. "He says that now. He didn't think it then," she added in a light tone.

Angelo chuckled but a seriousness returned to his face quickly. "Bianca told me you two have been seeing each other a lot."

Though Mara sent him a withering look, the effort was futile.

On he went. "Bianca can't decide if that's good or bad. She wants you happy," he said as an excuse, finally noticing Mara's frown. "That's what we all want."

"What do we all want?" Bianca piped in.

"You to keep quiet once in a while," Nick gibed.

Rick hadn't even been aware of Mara's brother's approaching.

"You're a sweetie," Bianca returned, pinching her brother's cheek none too gently.

Nick shifted a look at Rick. "Glad you came."

Too many years in the newspaper business made Rick doubt that comment. Mara's brother wouldn't have gone from suspicious and wary to welcoming and friendly that fast.

"Mara just told me you used to work on a newspaper. Where?"

Bianca elbowed her brother in the ribs. "Stop that. This is a party. Quit playing Dirty Harry."

Unfazed by his sister's reprimand, Nick shrugged. "Bianca, you're just peeved because you want to ask questions."

"That's not true," she protested.

"Sure it is."

"What is this?" Mara's mother nudged her way between her son and son-in-law.

Rick gathered the affectionate sniping between brother and sister ranked as an enjoyable pastime for them.

"Nick's picking on me, Mama," Bianca complained, but laughed.

Not looking a bit contrite, Nick snickered. "You've been saying that since you were old enough to talk."

"No, I haven't. I've been saying it since you were old enough to talk."

"Jerk," she shot back at him and hooked her arm in her husband's to urge him away. They moved only inches before Uncle Luigi bear-hugged Bianca.

"Nick and Bianca really do love each other," Mara assured Rick.

Though overwhelmed by the affectionate displays around him, Rick envied the closeness among family members. "It shows."

Mara drew away to open the refrigerator. Humor brightened her voice. "They always entertained me when we were kids."

Rick visually swept the room from his position behind the island counter in the kitchen. "You didn't get involved in it?"

"I was the baby. Bianca has played little mother to me since I was born, according to Mama. And Nick's protective streak kept several of my boyfriends in line. I always wondered why none of them ever wanted to park and neck with me. I learned from one of them that my big brother promised to break both of his arms if he touched anything but my hand."

Rick turned a squinty-eyed look back at her. "Should I consider myself lucky that he didn't make that threat to me?"

"He wouldn't dare." Mara rummaged in a drawer for the bottle opener. "I'm bigger now." She set the beer before him. "He knows I'd hit him."

Facing her, he watched while she scooped the coffee grounds into the basket of the huge coffee urn. "But he still protects you."

"Yes, he does. More so, since Steve. Trust comes slowly for them," she said, looking away to plug in the coffeepot. "I'm the easy one."

Wasn't it that knowledge that made his own deception more foul? She trusted, and he was betraying her—not with lies, but an omission of truth.

"Mara, where did you put the Scrabble game?" Bianca called out from across the room.

"I'll get it." She touched Rick's shoulder. "I guess it's time to quiet the kids."

"How would anyone notice?" he remarked as the noise level rose to a deafening buzz.

Mara stepped away on a laugh, pleased he seemed to be enjoying himself.

For the next few minutes, Rick nursed his beer and observed. When he was a reporter, he'd spent a lot of time watching people for some telltale gesture that indicated they'd like to tell their story. Among the gregarious crowd cramped in Mara's small living room, everyone reveled in sharing their thoughts and opinions.

"You can't stay in this corner all night," Mara's mother scolded, smiling. Though she'd plumped with age, she had the same beauty, the same flawless complexion and sparkling dark eyes as her daughter.

"Would you believe I'm enjoying myself watching everyone?"

"Yes." Her smile intensified with good-natured warmth. "We have our share of people who others might view as odd."

Rick recognized she possessed a teasing manner similar to Mara's. "I'd say interesting, not odd."

Looking amused, Teresa arched an eyebrow. "You're very kind." Her eyes grew more intense, as if trying to see inside him. "But we learned that about you already." She beamed at him now. "Our daughter is happier than she's been in over year, except when Jessie was born."

At that moment, Rick felt like hell. So much trust was being offered, and he warranted none of it.

"Mama," Bianca interrupted, standing on the other side of the counter. "Papa wants you."

Instead of stepping away, Bianca stalled until her mother was out of hearing range. "Let me give you a warning."

Rick prepared himself for a sister's protective lecture. He didn't need one. He knew how vulnerable Mara was. In her mind, trust and love went hand in hand. If she offered love, she did it without boundaries.

"You have to eat a lot," Bianca insisted and grinned, "or the family will think you don't like them."

Rick forced a smile. If only he'd met these people before his life had been turned upside down. "I'll stuff myself."

"A wise decision," Mara's father broke in. Bouncing Jessie in his arms, Vito nudged his daughter with an elbow. "Bianca, go tell Mara your good news."

Rick glanced at the cake and the number propped on top of it. "You've been married thirty-five years?"

"Good years, too. We've had our troubles, but trouble shared is easier," he said meaningfully.

Rick straightened from his relaxed pose. Had they all guessed he had his allotment of it?

"Toast," Uncle Luigi announced.

Mara's father shrugged. "My public calls me. Now, where is my wife?" he said with a quick visual sweep of the room. "Ah, it's time to rescue her from my sister. Gina's a wonderful woman. But bossy," he added on a chuckle at his own words before he weaved his way to his wife.

"To Teresa and Vito," Luigi yelled, quieting conversations.

As glasses were raised, the words echoed around the room.

Regret filled Rick. Staring at Mara's parents, he knew that love meant sharing everything. Unless he was honest with Mara, he had to leave.

Spotting her, he maneuvered his way around Mara's Aunt Gina and three kids sprawled on the floor playing Scrabble, but halfway across the room, he was stopped twice. Mara's brother-in-law shared his view about the city's hockey team having a winning streak, and to Rick's amazement, Mara's brother joined them, even suggesting a guys' night out.

Caught in conversation with two cousins, Mara watched Rick inching his way to reach her. She backed away to meet him halfway. "I wish we were alone," she whispered, catching his hand.

"Later?"

"Oh, yes, later," she assured him. She wanted to kiss him, to announce to everyone how important he was to her. All night she'd watched her family seeking him out, and with every encounter, smiles had been exchanged. Just as she'd hoped, they liked him. They really liked him. "Is my family ganging up on you?"

"Not at all." He could have told her that they'd all been kind. Everyone had made him feel welcome, even Mara's brother. It was more than he'd expected. As he stood, surrounded by her family and lifelong friends, he realized she was part of a world he might never know. When he'd agreed to enter the Witness Security Program, he'd never envisioned how much he might really have to give up. Then Mara had entered his life—and Jessie. He'd bonded with both of them almost from the start. Besides feelings of affection, a need to protect them overwhelmed him. It was as if they were his child, his wife. Ironically, the one he needed to protect them from the most was himself.

"They won't leave you alone," Mara warned. Amusement danced in her eyes. "As you should have guessed, because of how I am, we're a pesty bunch."

He smiled with her. "You look happy. Has something happened?"

"Yes. Something wonderful." She beamed, sliding an arm around his waist as if the gesture were as natural as breathing. "My sister and her husband have decided to adopt. I think that's great news. They want a baby so badly." She cast a glance at Bianca, who was laughing despite a rather pale look. Mara had stopped her earlier, concerned.

"It's only the flu, I think," Bianca had said, but had looked too ebullient for someone sick. That was when she'd told her that they were going to an adoption agency. "It could take forever," she'd added, as if trying to quell her own excitement. "They check everything, but it's going to happen. We'll have a cousin for Jessie to play with."

Mara had hugged her, had wanted to shout to anyone who would listen what great parents Bianca and Angelo would be.

"Where are you?" Rick asked, tipping his head to see her face.

"Thinking how lucky I am." As family members crowded around the table for slices of cake, she stepped away from him to play hostess.

Rick wandered to a window and stared out at the darkness. He saw nothing. For too long, he'd felt nothing. Now, so much of what he needed in his life was within his grasp. And it scared the hell out of him as he realized how easily, how quickly it might all slip away.

Across the room, Mara cut the cake, passing good-natured comments to family members requesting either itsy-bitsy slices or man-size ones, but a restlessness rushed over her. What she wanted was to be near Rick. She loved him without reservation. Was she being foolish? she wondered as her brother's words returned. Why hadn't Nick been able to learn anything about him? Why did she feel that despite how open Rick was with her, he kept a portion of himself from her? Maybe she imagined that. Coming from her family, she was used to people saying everything they thought and felt. There was nothing mysterious about him, she convinced herself. He was simply different from them. That's all.

Certain that everyone had cake, Mara took a plate for herself. Her cousin Carmen, the family shutterbug, began snapping photos. Stella, no longer jealous, posed for several before he began circling the room and issuing instructions to family members to smile.

Mara poked a fork into the soft frosting and smiled as laughter rose in response to her cousin Perry hamming it up.

"He's always been the family clown," her mother said.

Mara nodded but said nothing, suddenly distracted. As Carmen neared Rick and Angelo, Rick stepped away before he was trapped in a family photo. He escaped only a few feet when Aunt Gina corralled him.

Her hands constantly moving, she rambled on about how her little brother had met Mara's mother thirty-five years ago. But the moment Carmen closed in on them with his camera, Rick eased away to disappear into another room.

"No daydreaming," Aunt Gina chided, snapping Mara's attention away from him. "You still have guests." She enveloped Mara in her arms. "It's a wonderful party, Mara."

Fiercely, Mara clung to the pleasure she'd been feeling all night. She didn't want doubts to creep in about Rick. Whether or not she was playing the ostrich and hiding her head in the sand, rather than facing doubt, she didn't care. After so long of pretending to be happy when she wasn't, she couldn't stand the idea of letting real joy slip away. Not now, especially not now, when he'd already told her he loved her.

Chapter Thirteen

Mara awoke with a start and fought to orient herself. As the alarm shrilled annoyingly, she groped to bang the snooze button. With the silence again, she snuggled deeper under the sheet and shifted to curl closer to Rick, but the strong, hard body that had warmed her during the night eased away. Lazily, Mara stretched. If she stayed in bed, she would fall behind in a schedule she'd forced herself to make. It allowed her time to set up the coffee brewer before she had to feed and dress Jessie and get ready for work. With her eyes closed, she remembered today wasn't a workday. A few more minutes of sleep wouldn't hurt.

She wasn't sure how much time passed. She drifted awake as the rich aroma of coffee wafted to her. Untangling herself from the sheet, she opened her eyes.

Sitting on the edge of the bed, Rick held a cup of coffee and grinned at her in a way that she was becoming familiar with. "For you."

With his warm gaze on her, in a self-conscious move Mara raked fingers through her messed hair. "Oh, you're wonderful."

"And you're beautiful." He satisfied himself with stroking the strands tousled from sleep. "And tempting," he said, marveling that the softness beneath his fingers was as silky as he once had imagined.

Pleasure sweeping through her, she pushed herself up and jammed a pillow behind her back. Instead of accepting the coffee, she coiled her arms around his neck. "You're spoiling me." Feather light, her tongue traced a slow path around the shell of his ear.

"You need some spoiling," he said on a laugh as she pressed herself against him. Warm and naked, she was inviting. "You watch out for everyone else."

"Just Jessie."

"And your parents and your sister and every tenant in this building."

"Only when they need it." Mara drew back to sip the steaming brew.

Admiration for her had been the first emotion she'd stirred in him. He still felt it whenever he considered how much responsibility she bore on slender shoulders. "And what do you need?"

Smiling, she caressed his head. "I have what I need."

For a long moment, he fixed intense-looking eyes on her. "If you can't think of anything, I'll have to for you."

A deeper smile tugged at her lips in response to the lightness in his voice. "Like what?"

Amused by the anticipation on her face, he stretched the tease. "That's my secret."

"Tell me." She pressed her lips to the curve of his neck, more because she was yearning for this closeness to continue than to persuade him. "You know that I can't stand secrets."

"Not even good ones?" With her peering over the rim of her cup at him, worry rocketed through Rick as he thought again about what needed to be said. "What about surprises?"

The thoughtful look in his eyes bothered her. What was troubling him? she wondered not for the first time. "Is something—" Jessie's wail silenced her. Pushing concern aside, Mara grinned wryly. "There's my wake-up call." She twisted her upper body toward the bedside table to set her cup on it.

Plagued by vacillating thoughts since awakening, Rick needed a few moments alone. He placed his palm under her cup, stopping her. "I'll get Jessie," he said, giving her a quick kiss before he backed off the bed.

His conscience nagged him during the walk from one bedroom to the next. Leaving was no longer an option. He wanted to stay, plan a future with her. To do that, he had to tell her everything.

Entering the nursery, Rick soothed Jessie. "Easy. It's okay." He winced at her penetrating cry and bent over the crib to pick her up. Eyes squeezed tight, her mouth trembling with each wail, she shook her arms and kicked her legs.

"Hey, hey," Rick murmured and lifted her into his arms. Gently he patted her bottom the way Mara did it. Within seconds she quieted, her mouth sucking furiously on the pacifier he'd offered her.

"If you can hold off, I'll get you into a clean diaper." What he was saying couldn't have mattered as much as the tone of his voice.

The pacifier appeased her while he inched tiny legs and feet out of the sleeper with its design of pink and white elephants.

Changing a diaper got easier with experience. After his brief baby-sitting duty, he considered himself a master at the task. Of course, he'd yet to remove a smelly diaper.

He used one of the moist wipes from a box in a side shelf of the dressing table. Jessie smiled behind the pacifier, not the least perturbed by the coolness on her skin.

The only nursery rhyme he knew was the one about Jack and Jill and a bucket of water. Though he whistled in the shower, he rarely sang in public except when drunk. But he sang the rhyme to her while he lathered pink lotion on her bottom and secured the diaper.

Jessie spit out the pacifier. With bright eyes fixed on him, she jabbered a combination of sounds at him.

"What are you trying to say to me, sweetheart?"

As a smile lit up her face again, warmth spread through his gut and chest. Every time she smiled, she made him forget anything that was wrong in his life.

Little fingers caught one of his and gripped tightly as if her life depended on it. His heart squeezed with emotion so intense he could barely breathe. "I love you, too," he said softly.

Rick cuddled her against his shoulder and ran a soothing hand over the back of her head. Lately, when he wandered into the same room, she recognized him. She would smile at him, talk to him. She made him feel as if he were an important part of her world. No, she wasn't his. Some other man was her biological father, some other man should be enjoying her smile, he tried to remember. But he didn't want to. He thought of Jessie as his own. He was the one who really loved her and her mother.

Mara touched a finger to her lips. They still carried the warmth from Rick's lips. Desperately, she'd wanted to ask, will you always be around? She shied away from the question, uneasy about challenging what they'd found together.

Head down, she shifted to place her feet on the floor. Then she heard Jessie's cooing.

From the doorway, Rick flashed a smile at her. "I changed her but thought you would want to feed her," he said, dangling a bottle in the hand cupped beneath Jessie's bottom.

Tenderness and love mingled within Mara. She was so lucky. It frightened her how lucky she felt since she'd found him.

Rick perched on the bed beside her and placed Jessie in her mother's arms.

"If this was your surprise, it's a nice one."

He wanted to smile because she was. "Ever had a picnic on the roof?"

Mara glanced away from Jessie's sucking to meet his gaze. "In winter?"

"Why not?" Coward, a voice in his head yelled. He knew he was stalling and why. He was worried that once she learned the truth, she wouldn't understand. "A lunchtime picnic. It's sunny outside. If you bundle Jessie, she'll be warm enough."

Mara sagged against the viselike band of his arm at her back. She'd imagined a moment like this, holding her baby and being held by the man she loved. After her marriage had ended, she'd thought it would never happen. But here she was with someone who loved her and Jessie. "I'm as adventurous as you are."

He smiled at the recognizable sensuality in her voice. "I know."

"Are you sure you don't want to have a picnic here?" Mara asked in a playful tone.

Rick arched an eyebrow. "Right here?" His lips curved in a slow, enticing smile. "In the bed?"

Mara rode with his humor. "Right here."

Unable to do more at the moment, he gave her a whispery kiss. "A picnic in the snow is a dumb idea, isn't it?"

Against his lips, Mara murmured, "Very dumb."

Tenderly he skimmed a finger down her cheek.

"Now, summer picnics on the lake are different." Enthusiasm sparkled in her eyes. "When I was young, I used to go to Montrose Beach a lot."

Rick narrowed his eyes. "Who was the guy?"

She nudged his ribs with her elbow. "Always with my family. Do you think the overprotective Vincettis would let the baby of the family parade around in a bathing suit and be alone with some guy?''

Rick grinned wryly. "So your whole family went?" he asked, visualizing the Vincetti clan in full force taking over a section of the beach.

"All of us. We had so much fun whenever we all got together." She laughed softly. "There was always too much food. Sometimes I was so stuffed I was sure I'd sink when I went in the water. We'd play volleyball, and the kids would have a watermelon-seed spitting contest.''

With a fingertip, Rick tucked a strand of hair behind her ear. "Did you ever win it?"

"No, Nick did." A smile curved the corners of her lips. "He'd boast for days after." Looking up at him, Mara patted Jessie gently on the back. "You'll love going to the beach." Immediately she wanted to bite her tongue. Was she presuming too much? Though he'd told her he loved her, he'd never indicated a future for them.

Rick felt her tense beside him. He wished uncertainties didn't exist between them. When she'd shared a memory of the Vincettis gathering at the beach, she'd drawn him in. He'd never been on a family picnic. Vaguely he recalled his own fifth birthday party, a red-haired kid named Jimmy and a new blue bicycle. With his father's death, he'd lost all sense of family. Mara had brought him into hers and made him remember how at peace someone could feel surrounded by people who were trusted.

"What are you doing?" She inclined her head to place it in his vision.

Rick shot her a puzzled look.

Uneasy at his unexpected quietness, Mara chose a tease. "Daydreaming?"

As she curled into him, he kissed her cheek. He found his face buried in the sweet-scented mass of her hair. The fragrance lured him as much as her touch had while they'd made love. "Remembering last night," he finally answered.

"Good thoughts?"

"You have to ask?" Tenderness, love and fear mingled within him. The sharp, conflicting emotions weighed him down because so much remained questionable for them. He tugged her tighter to him. "Fantastic ones," he answered before reluctantly slipping his arm from her. "I'll shower and be back." Rick pushed to a stand and stared at her and Jessie. They'd given him what really mattered most.

"Soon?" Mara asked with as much lightness as she could muster as she noticed his frown.

At her inquiring look, he strained for a laugh to stir one from her. "Before you're dressed. So don't rush doing it."

Mara raised an eyebrow. "Oh?"

Bracing his arms on either side of her, he leaned forward. "Think Jessie will go back to sleep?"

"Unlikely," Mara returned, stroking his cheek and raising her face for another kiss.

Instead of a brief one, he let his mouth linger and drew a soft sigh from her. "I'll be back in a few minutes." He was gutless, he decided as he ambled to his apartment. He couldn't find the backbone to tell her everything. It wasn't that he didn't trust her. He had more faith in her than anyone else. But what would the truth bring them? Would she understand why he'd lied to her all this time? That question threateningly hung like a rope around his neck.

Rick took a quick shower, dressed, then slid the pages of his manuscript into an envelope. Dangling it and a copy for her to read, he wondered if he'd still be at the apartment when he received a reply about it. Would he ever know if he had what it took to be a writer?

In midstride, he stilled as the top stair before the landing squeaked. Mara was in her apartment, caring for Jessie. No one in her family would visit so early in the morning. No one.

Despite all of Carl's precautions, had Van's men located him? Though he'd strived for optimism, deep down Rick figured it was only a matter of time before Van found him again.

He hadn't wanted to listen to Carl when he'd suggested another move. In a way, he might have been fooling himself, believing he was done running. At the moment, it occurred to him that he might never be.

He shot a look at the telephone as a thought formed to call Carl. Hell, what if he was being paranoid again? What if it was Ernie, the building's maintenance man?

What if it wasn't? Van's retribution could come in an instant. He listened and heard another squeak. Outside his door? he wondered. With silent steps, he approached it. He was damn sick and tired of running, he realized, and quietly unlocked the door to turn the knob.

* * *

Mara clicked the last snap on Jessie's sleeper and lifted her into her arms. Ambling into the kitchen, she considered what she had in her refrigerator for their picnic. A trip to the restaurant might be needed. Crusty bread, cheese, a bottle of wine and . . .

The thought died as Mara heard a noise in the hallway. She listened for only a moment. A male voice yelled, then she heard scuffling.

Rounding the kitchen counter, she scooted back into the bedroom to set Jessie in her crib. Though she rushed to her door, she wasn't stupid. A woman alone had to show some caution. So she peeked out.

His back to her, Rick had pinned someone against the wall. Mara hurried out to the hall. "What's happening? Do you want me to call the police?"

The last thing Rick wanted was police involved. Keeping a grip on the guy's shirt collar, Rick assessed him quickly. He appeared too clean-cut to be involved with Van. And physically, he was too soft. "No." Rick remained planted over the guy. "What were you doing here, sneaking around?" he demanded.

Mara craned her neck to see. In shock, she stared down at the flushed face of her ex-husband.

At her gasp, Steve swung a wide-eyed look at her over Rick's shoulder. "Mara, get help," he appealed.

Rick turned a puzzled look on her. "You know him?

As though she'd been running too fast, she drew a hard breath. "Rick, this is Steve."

Free from Rick's grasp, a pale Steve glowered at Mara. "Who the hell is this?" he asked angrily, jabbing an arm in Rick's direction.

Mara shook her head in disbelief. This couldn't be happening.

"Who the hell are you?" Steve yelled at Rick.

"Shh," Mara insisted. "This can't go on," she said quietly. "You'll wake up the whole building if you keep yelling like that."

"Fine." Steve snagged her arm. "Let's go in. I want to talk to you."

Rick saw red. With a quick side step, he blocked the path to the door. "Take your hand off her."

"This is my wife."

"Ex-wife." Rick measured out his words with chilling slowness. "Take your hand off her."

Steve met him with an air of defiance. "I'll do what I damn well please."

"Like hell," Rick said and took a step closer.

"Take it easy." Steve raised hands in front of him as if prepared to ward off a punch. "I only want to talk to you, Mara," Steve appealed.

Because there seemed no other alternative, Mara opened her door. "Come in."

As Steve stepped forward, so did Rick.

"Now just a minute," Steve flared, turning back to Rick. "This is private, and you..."

"I'm staying." Mara was sure Rick was stifling a renewed wave of anger.

Steve's frown deepened. "Mara, we need to talk."

"I'll make sure that's all you do," Rick broke in.

Briefly his gaze shifted to Mara as if silently questioning her. Though she felt she could handle Steve, too much had passed between her and Rick to turn down his willingness to be there if she needed him. "He's coming in, too," Mara announced finally.

Steve's back went rigid. "Who is he to you?" he demanded, gesturing with his thumb at Rick.

"A friend," she answered because that was the truth. "A good friend." Her eyes strayed to Rick again. "A special one."

"Well, isn't that dandy." Steve's sarcasm won him their full attention.

Mara laughed mirthlessly. "Please, don't play the betrayed one," she warned.

Rick inched closer to her. Placing an envelope on an end table, he braced his backside against the arm of the sofa, and physically delivered a message. If Steve had plans to bully her, he would lose.

As if sensing the danger lurking near if he challenged her, Steve mercly shrugged. "I'm going to ignore him."

Mara nearly smiled. That was no easy task. At better than six feet, Rick easily towered over him.

Steve zeroed in on her again. "Mara, I've only come because I want to talk. When I called, you were acting like a stubborn..." He shot a nervous glance in Rick's direction. "Well, you were stubborn," he said instead of finishing his original sentence. "Let's sit down, babe, and talk calmly," he requested, flashing a smile.

Mara stayed on her feet. "Talk." He wasn't welcome in her apartment. If he thought she would sit with him like an old friend, he was badly mistaken.

"Okay, have it your way," he said resignedly. "But there's no need for you to be so difficult."

Mara heaved a sigh, realizing how much she wanted to snap at him. "Am I doing that?"

"Look, you know I never planned on being a father."

"So you said before you left." She thought about another woman, pregnant by him, and felt sympathy for her. "Too bad you never mentioned that before I got pregnant."

A crooked grin touched his handsome face. "Guess we should have discussed that." He laughed in a way that held no humor. "I can't deal with it, Mara. I know you wanted a baby. You'll be good with her."

Tension coiled around Mara like a tight spring. "What are you saying?"

"I felt smothered at the idea that it wouldn't be the two of us anymore."

Jerk, Rick mused.

"Why are you here?" Mara asked, growing impatient with him.

"I lost my job. Now I've started a new life. I'm engaged, but we're living with her mother because money is tight. So how can I give you any?"

Rick wanted to punch the dumb smile off his face.

Mara had had too many problems of her own since Steve had split to feel any compassion.

"I won't bother with custody, Mara—" Steve gave Rick an uncertain look "—if you don't ask for child support," he said so softly it almost seemed as if he were trying to whisper the words.

Mara recognized that she would do anything to get him out of her life forever. "All right."

He smiled in that slow, charming way that she supposed was meant to make her regret he wasn't with her anymore. To her, he simply looked smug, so smug she wanted to hit him.

"And you'll have to pay off the bills because I don't have a job or any—"

"Money, I know," Mara cut in impatiently and moved toward the door to urge him in that direction.

As if everything was right with the world again, he grinned and took several steps. Suddenly he stopped.

Now what? Mara wondered, placing her hand on her stomach as muscles tightened.

"I guess I should see her," Steve said as if some sense of his obligation hit him.

It amazed Mara that she'd ever loved him, that they'd made such a beautiful daughter, that he lacked so much sensitivity. "Don't bother, Steve," she returned with a remarkable amount of calm under the circumstances.

"If that's the way you want it." He shrugged indifferently, revealing no sincerity or need to see the child he'd fathered.

"Yes, it is." She felt fury but no pain. Closing the door behind him, she sighed with relief. He meant nothing to her anymore. It's over, she told herself. She'd ended her life with him.

Rick watched her back straighten, then curled a hand around her shoulder. He felt an unmistakable tenseness in her body as the small of her back seemed to draw forward. "You let him off the hook."

"I'd hate for Jessie to expect anything from him, to be lied to by him and then let down. That would hurt her more than never knowing him."

"I'm sorry." Rick felt at a loss for words. There were too many he wanted to say, but he kept them to himself because they'd only vent his anger and not help her.

"I won, Rick." Her eyes locked with his. "Believe me. I'm the winner. So is Jessie."

Rick managed a slim smile. After the deadbeat jerk she called an ex-husband had stomped on her trust and their vows with his deceit, she would expect no secrets from the person she loved.

At his silence, Mara tilted her head. In his eyes, she thought she saw uncertainty. Because of Steve? She wanted to soothe, to assure him. Most of all, she wanted the laughter back that they'd shared earlier that morning. "Let me get Jessie bundled, and we'll go to the restaurant for food for our picnic."

Rick felt her need for some calm. For both their sakes, it might be best to wait with what he needed to say until the turmoil from her ex-husband's visit had subsided completely. Another hour or two. He wanted that with her before the questions began, before the light in her eyes diminished when she looked at him.

Mara took a step and spotted the mailing envelope he'd put on the end table when he'd come in. "You're mailing the manuscript today?"

He saw an eagerness in her eyes to be part of this with him. "Before I chicken out," he admitted.

"Strong, brave men aren't supposed to admit such a thing," she teased.

"Did I ruin my image?"

"You enhanced it," she assured him with a smile.

Mara's plan to breeze in and out of the restaurant was thwarted the moment the door closed behind her and Rick. Customers were backed up in the line, others waited for tables to be cleared. Mara scanned her family's faces and read stress in each of them. She also noticed Bianca was missing. Taking Jessie from Rick, she scurried to her mother, only waiting until she'd finished making change for a customer before asking the obvious question: "You're short-handed?"

"Bianca called and said she would be late, and then this." Her mother's hand fluttered in the air before she gestured at the crowded restaurant. "I forgot today was the Saint Patrick's Day parade. That was good and bad for us. Lots of business. People get hungry, watching parades."

"I'll help."

"No," her mother protested. "It's your day off."

Mara shifted Jessie to her other arm. "Bianca's coming in, isn't she?"

Her mother nodded while making change for another customer.

"I'll stay until she does." Not waiting for a response, Mara placed Jessie in the playpen that was tucked in a corner of the kitchen, then hurried back to Rick, who was ordering coffee. "I won't be long," she said after quickly summarizing her family's problem. Lightly, she touched his jaw. "I promise."

And I promise to level with you. He kept the words to himself for now. After giving him so much, would she understand? Until he'd met her, he hadn't known what being a part of a family really meant. And he hadn't realized how much he ached for the family she had, for the family she offered, for someone like her. Everything Rick valued hung in the balance, depending on his ability to make her believe that some deception was necessary.

Positioning himself so he had a full view of the customers walking in, he settled at a table near the door, facing it. He'd nearly finished the coffee when the jingle of the bell above the door made him look up from the dark brew in his cup.

With a weary smile, Carl lumbered toward him, his eyebrows bunched with his frown. Uneasiness spread through Rick. Every anxious moment he'd had intensified. Something was wrong. Carl wouldn't have come looking for him otherwise.

"I took a chance that I'd find you here." Carl sank to the chair across from him. "We just had a close one."

Rick didn't want to hear this.

"We tailed a guy yesterday from your workplace to your apartment building."

Yesterday Rick had been with Mara. That had saved his life. But then, she'd been responsible for changing it from the first moment he'd met her.

"When we picked him up, he wasn't shy about admitting he worked for Van, had the contract on you. Of course, we used a little persuasion. If he cooperated, we'd go easier on an outstanding burglary charge."

Rick readied himself for Carl's next words. "So now what?" He traced Mara's stare to them. At any moment, Rick expected her to come to the table to say hello to Carl. "I leave again?" he asked, his attention shifting back to Carl.

"You go nowhere," Carl said on a gruff laugh. "Van's not going to get a trial."

Rick thought he'd misunderstood. "He dropped his appeal?"

"A guard found him in the laundry workroom this morning. He's dead. Heart attack. It's over, Eric."

Rick spotted Bianca, rushing to her parents. Nearby, Mara delivered sodas to a table. How much could she hear? he wondered. A few moments alone with her was all he needed to tell her the truth.

Carl cocked his head and grinned. "You don't look as relieved as I expected. Are you having trouble believing what I've told you? It's finally come to an end, Eric." His voice trailed off as he looked beyond Rick.

Rick swiveled a look over his shoulder.

"Eric?" With a tray of dishes in her hands, Mara stared in puzzlement at him. "Is your real name Eric?"

Why now? Rick wanted to yell. This was the wrong way to tell her. With a few more minutes, he could offer her everything he ached to give her. Carl had handed him his freedom, and all that he had believed was impossible was within his reach.

A small thing, Mara told herself. Lots of people used nicknames. She tried out his name. "Eric Sloan.

I might need a little while to get used to it,'' she said lightly.

As Carl stood to leave, Mara started to protest. She'd been pleased to see Carl again, was planning to bring her mother to their table, introduce Carl to her family.

Carl's next words halted her. "It was a pleasure meeting you, Mara. Goodbye."

Dumbfounded, Mara visually followed him until the door closed behind him. "His goodbye sounded so final."

Pushing back his chair, Rick rose and reached for the tray of dirty dishes she held. "Mara, sit down."

Not his words, but the seriousness in his eyes made her drop to the chair across from him.

"He's not a relative," Rick announced, setting down the tray. "And my name isn't Eric Sloan. It's Lassiter. Eric Lassiter."

Chapter Fourteen

Was she breathing? She wasn't sure. Confusion sweeping over her, she studied his face, searching for answers. "What are you talking about?"

Rick closed a hand over hers, needing the contact. "I'm not who I said I was. I couldn't tell you more. I wanted to, but I couldn't tell you."

"Tell me," Mara repeated faintly, trying not to think too much, not to jump to conclusions. "Why couldn't you?"

"Because I was never sure I would stay."

"So you—you lied to me?"

As she shook her head in the manner of someone trying to clear her mind of muddled thoughts, he rushed words to stop what might happen if he didn't. "Let me explain."

A slowly building ache rose inside her. Steve had used those same words before he admitted all of his lies to her. She knew now that Rick had kept his real name from her, and he'd told her Carl was a relative. What else had been a lie? "I made the same mistake, didn't I?" she asked incredulously.

Rick reached forward but hesitated, certain she would shun his touch. "I'm sorry. I told you as much of the truth as possible."

A deep unbelievable pain stabbed her. She still didn't understand. She'd made love with him. She'd left her baby with him, but he couldn't tell her about whatever was happening in his life. "But not all of the truth?"

"I gave as much of it as I could."

She bowed her head and shook it. "I'm such a fool."

"You're not."

How could he say she wasn't when it was so clear to her? Her voice was laced with the pain of her own realization. "I loved you. And I trusted you. I believed what you told me. I defended you to my family. I was so sure of you, so certain you were being truthful with me."

"I had no business getting involved with you. Or falling in love with you. But I couldn't stop myself. You gave me more of a reason to keep going. Before, I was simply surviving. I found with you all I ever wanted."

Mara struggled with a desire to believe him. In a way, she did. She believed he loved her. But she'd gone through a scene like this before. She'd been made a fool then. She'd believed in someone who'd lied to her.

"Mara, I couldn't tell you," he said angrily, but lowered his voice as a few heads turned in their direction. She didn't understand, didn't realize what had been at stake and wouldn't until she knew everything. "I was hanging on to my life by my fingertips."

His words made her realize she couldn't switch off the love she felt for him. "You've been in danger?" she asked. But of course he had. That explained how wary he'd been, how suspicious he sometimes seemed.

"I was. Not anymore."

Emotions warred inside her. What good was a love that didn't include honesty? "Love is nothing without trust. And no matter what you say now, you never trusted me."

"Damn. Yes, I trusted you."

"But not enough to tell me, to share with me any of whatever it was that was wrong." She pulled back suddenly as if he'd slapped her. "Not enough to be truthful."

Rick sucked in a breath as accusation dulled her dark eyes. "I wanted to tell you."

"But you didn't." Blinking hard, she pushed to a stand.

He couldn't let it end like this. "Wait a minute." Rick snagged her wrist. "There's a lot you don't know."

Mara whirled on him. "Exactly. And whose fault is that?"

He gentled his hand on her. "I didn't know if we'd have a future," he tried to explain. He would make her listen. Hell, he would beg. He would do anything to make her understand. Too much was at risk for him to walk away now—now, when he could finally have all he wanted, all she'd offered, all they could share. "But I never pretended what I felt for you."

She wouldn't cry. Vincetti pride demanded that much of her. Mara tugged free of his grip. "It's not enough for me," she said with too much calm.

The chill in her voice kept him from stepping closer. She was remembering another man. And to her, he was no different, but he couldn't give up. He'd found too much with her and Jessie. "I can't forget you," Rick insisted.

"Then that's your problem." The wounded look in her eyes returned. "I've already forgotten you," she said before turning away. She didn't look back, afraid if she did, she would rush back into his arms.

Rick started to follow her, but her father blocked the entrance to the kitchen. Rick could have easily muscled his way past him, but he would only alienate the people he needed on his side the most. One glance at Teresa assured him that might never happen. Her dark eyes mirrored her daughter's. Watching the condemnation in them intensifying, he knew that the hurt was too fresh to reason with any of them, especially Mara.

As welcome as they had made him feel the night of the party, they shut him out now. Nothing he could say, no excuse, would carry enough weight to explain away what had seemed obvious to them. In some way, he'd shattered Mara's happiness.

After the pain Steve had inflicted on her, she'd vowed never to shed tears again over any man. She'd worked so hard to overcome heartache, to provide her baby with a confident, stable environment. She couldn't afford to be some weepy, sentimental fool.

For her daughter's sake, she couldn't relent. No explanation existed that would allow her to forget and forgive his dishonesty. If he lied once, what guaranteed he wouldn't again?

"He left, Mara."

As she lifted up Jessie, her father enveloped both of them in his arms. "Papa, will I ever stop being so easily taken in?"

With a deep sigh, he patted her back. "What did he say?"

"I didn't let him say anything. I couldn't. I remember how I clung to a hope with Steve that he would tell me something that would make sense, and I would find a way to save my marriage. Instead, he only fed me more lies."

His eyes saddened for her. "Could it be he wanted to protect you?"

Mara drew back, surprised at his defending Rick. With Steve, he'd been furious, not understanding. She took in a deep breath. "It wouldn't matter. I can't understand any reason to lie to someone you're supposed to love."

After a restless night, Mara awoke exhausted the following morning and dragged herself from bed. Jessie prevented her from burying her head beneath the pillow. Ambling into the sun-drenched kitchen, Mara flicked on the radio. Whatever she'd had with Rick was over. It was stupid to waste time reflecting on what had been and speculating over why everything between them had ended.

She concentrated on the heavy-metal music. That lasted only a second before she switched the dial to

Off. It was unlikely she would find serenity via screeching guitars.

She poured coffee but only held the cup. She didn't want to think about him and couldn't stop doing just that. It was her own fault. She'd walked away without knowing why he'd been leading a phony life. Anything unfinished went against a natural tendency within her that had always made her complete everything she'd started. Now she might never know.

Cradling the cup, she stared at the copy of Rick's manuscript that he'd left for her to read. With a desperateness she wished she didn't feel, she hoped the words would reveal something to help her comprehend. She picked up one page and began to skim it, then returned to the beginning and read each word. Page after page engrossed her more. The story was filled with one man's torment as he seesawed between his duty to justice and truth and the consequences on his life because of those scruples. The words held her spellbound.

She stopped only to pour herself a cup of coffee and take care of Jessie's needs. Hours passed, and she ached, because instead of understanding him better, she was more confused. Even as she lost herself in his story, by the time she finished reading, she was racked with puzzlement. One question lingered after she read the last page. How could he express so much perception, be so sensitive to the feelings of his characters, portray a man so bound by his personal ethics, yet mislead her without a second thought?

After leaving the restaurant, Rick had walked aimlessly, then taken a night flight to Miami. While other passengers had slept, he'd tried to come to terms with everything. Overnight his life had changed. He guessed he could get his old job back in Miami, but there was nothing for him there. Everyone he cared about was in Chicago. And for the first time in his life, he knew the pain of missing someone.

Through the next day, he handled business that he'd left in limbo when he'd made his exodus nearly a year ago. He learned a friend had stored his possessions in his basement and, because of grief, had left everything there even after notification of Rick's death. Rick spent the day with him and his wife and collected his books but left the baseball autographed by Mickey Mantle for his buddy.

A trip to his old employer meant hours of explanation. Rick spent the week writing the story of his past year's experience for his editor, and nixed the idea of working for him again. He had other plans. At the moment he wasn't certain how successful he would be with all of them. But only one really mattered.

He entered his Chicago apartment close to midnight on the following Monday. He passed the next morning securing a new job at a Chicago newspaper. This was his home now. Whether or not he would find all he ever wanted depended on one woman.

As Mara had done every morning since she'd last seen Rick, she breezed past his apartment door and down the stairs. Because of the silence from across the hall during the previous week, she assumed he'd left town. Mrs. Torrence claimed he hadn't notified her of subleasing his apartment.

For what seemed the umpteenth time, Mara told herself that she didn't care what he did. Carrying Jessie in her arms, Mara entered the restaurant for work. No matter how much her heart ached about Rick, she was a Vincetti. For Jessie and for her family's sake, she'd curbed emotions during the past week, convincing herself that she had a life before without Rick. And she would have one again.

She went through the motions at the restaurant, managing weak smiles at the right moments, but her mother's gaze held doubt and her father's offered concern.

After settling Jessie in her playpen, she tied on an apron to begin kitchen work.

"Mara, a phone call for you," her cousin called from the front of the restaurant.

Mara sidestepped a delivery man carrying several cases of soda and wound a path toward the phone. She noticed Bianca had arrived, later than usual, and had cornered their parents near the cash register. Something important must have happened. Her mouth moved nonstop.

"Who's on the phone?" Mara asked Tony as she approached.

He shrugged indifferently and turned away to stack loaves of bread on a shelf.

For a second she dropped her guard, hoping it was Rick.

Instead, Mara's lawyer answered her greeting. "Your ex-husband has agreed to handle the payment for the bills he made."

Mara held her breath, frightened at what hadn't been said yet. What had Steve demanded? Custody rights for a child he hadn't wanted, had never even cared to see? "What was his reaction?"

"Resigned, actually. He relinquished his rights. I told him, as you requested, that you would make no demands for money in the future, if he agreed to that."

"Oh, thank you." She let relief drift over her. "Thank God. It's over then? I won't have any trouble with him?"

"He would be an idiot to cause any problems. You would have the upper hand."

"He's no fool," Mara returned. *I always was.*

"I'd say he was. But aren't you lucky that he is?"

Mara set down the receiver with a different attitude. She'd been feeling sorry for herself, feeling like a loser. Pride insisted differently. She'd weathered the failure of her marriage, had dodged the possibility of a difficult custody battle and her daughter wouldn't suffer from lack of love.

Ambling back to the kitchen, she scanned the work left to do and deliberately chose a particular task. Despite her quick pep talk, she wasn't certain she was as strong and determined as she wanted to believe. With emotions too close to the surface, if a thought of Rick flashed through her mind, she expected unwanted tears to flow.

Stationing herself before the chopping block, she snatched up an onion and began hacking at it vigorously. Mara minced the onion and sniffed, succumbing to a heat of tears behind her eyes.

With the sound of footsteps, she looked up to see her father's frown. Mara mustered a smile. "It's the onions," she said as an explanation for crying.

Despite his nod in passing, he hadn't looked reassured that her excuse was entirely truthful.

That her response hadn't been honest bothered her. Then she recalled what her father had said the other day. *You're a wise man, Papa.* To protect *him* from her sadness, she had uttered a slight fib.

"Mara, Mara!" Bianca waltzed up to her. "I've already told Mama and Papa." The brightness in her eyes vanished in an instant. "Are you crying?"

Mara held up an onion. "What have you told them?"

Elation spread across her sister's face again. "I took the test."

Sliding the diced onion into a stainless-steel bowl, Mara visually measured how many more she'd have to chop. "What test?"

"A home pregnancy test. I'm pregnant," she said excitedly, wrapping her arms around Mara. "I'm pregnant."

"Oh, Bianca." Mara squeezed her sister. "I'm so happy. This is wonderful."

"Isn't it?" She beamed at Mara, looking both jubilant and a little green.

"Today, I'll handle the food," Mara suggested.

Bianca laughed. "That might be a good idea." In a studying manner, her eyes met Mara's. "Are you okay?"

Though it wasn't easy, Mara managed a thin smile. "I'm fine."

As thrilled as she was for her sister, she wasn't fine.

"You look lousy," Nick said, stepping aside to let Bianca squeeze past him through the kitchen doorway.

Mara muttered an unladylike response that made him arch an eyebrow.

"Stop that damn chopping, will you?" He braced a shoulder against the wall. "You need to see something," he said and tossed a newspaper down on the counter in front of her.

As if in a trance, Mara stared at the front-page story about Eric Lassiter. Skimming the column, she felt her breathing growing more labored. A top-notch reporter, a winner of a press award for his investigative reporting, he had been a material witness in the Justice Department's case against Frank Van, a crime kingpin.

Mara murmured, "He went under cover working as a chauffeur for Van."

"Go on," Nick urged. "Read the rest."

Mara shook her head as her vision blurred from tears.

Her brother went on as if he'd memorized the story. "His investigation provided facts about drug connections between Van and Colombia. He was whisked to a safe house and placed in the Federal Witness Security Program. After the trial and his testimony, authorities set up a phony car accident in which he was supposed to have died. But he was given a new identity and relocated to Texas. That life lasted four months. When Frank Van's appeal for a new trial came through, Rick was sent here and given a new identity."

Mara sensed her brother had moved closer, but so many thoughts were barraging her mind.

Nick nudged back strands of her hair to see her face. "It can't be easy always looking over your shoulder."

"He admitted he'd been in danger," she said weakly, staring at the mound of chopped onions before her.

"Not anymore. Van is dead. Lassiter doesn't have to testify at a second trial, and the contract on him doesn't exist anymore." With a thumb, Nick brushed a tear streaking down her cheek. "That's one tough guy you're in love with," he said with admiration.

Nodding, Mara squeezed her eyes shut. "I can't believe it—I was so terrible to him."

Nick cleared his throat. "Ah, I think I win the award for that," he said lightly.

Mara couldn't respond to his amusement. She'd found a man whose only fault was honesty. He'd been so honest that he'd been willing to give up everything because of that integrity. Rick was nothing like her ex. "Oh, Nick."

"Easy," he soothed.

She couldn't stop berating herself. How could she when she'd insisted on trust from him, but she hadn't given it?

Rick stalled outside the restaurant. He planned on having his say. Because he couldn't blame anyone but himself for what had happened, guilt still rested heavily on him. But without her, he would have nothing. Pain spiraled through him whenever he thought of never seeing her again, not hearing her voice or her laughter.

Entering the restaurant, the first person he saw was Mara's brother. Rick took a split second to gear up for whatever was ahead. Her brother didn't bother him.

What he worried most about was seeing that despair in Mara's eyes again—a hurt he'd caused.

Mara lifted two pans of lasagna from the oven while her mother ladled Italian beef into one of the stainless-steel serving dishes. "Do you want help carrying this out to the front?" Mara asked before she set down the pot holders.

"I can handle them." Teresa eyed the chopping board. "Are you finished?"

"No, I'm sorry." Since she'd arrived she'd been dragging herself through even the simplest tasks. "I'll have it all done before lunch."

Teresa pressed her cheek to hers. "Did I ask that?"

Mara forced a laugh. "No, you didn't."

Nearby in her playpen, Jessie babbled at the mobile of pastel-colored elephants dancing in the air.

"Hey."

With a start, Mara and her mother jerked back from each other.

Nick grinned at both of them. "I heard Bianca's good news. That's great."

Teresa nodded. "Wonderful."

"Ah, I want to talk to you again," Nick said, closing the distance to Mara. He snatched a slice of green pepper from the cutting board. "I've never bugged you like the rest of the family has about dating guys I know. Right?" He didn't wait for her response. "But I know this guy who would be perfect for you."

Mara released an exasperated breath. "Not now, Nick," she practically pleaded.

"Nicholas," their mother said in a familiar reprimanding tone.

He held a halting hand up to her. "Mama, it's okay. Mara, I just want you to meet him. You don't have to go out with him."

Mara fought an urge to yell at him. Why wouldn't he take no for an answer?

"He's here—at the restaurant."

Threateningly, she eyed him. "The answer is no."

As if suddenly deaf, he went on, "I'll bring him back here so you can look him over."

"Nick!" she yelled, but he'd whirled away. She didn't need this now. She wanted to see one man, only one.

"Humor your brother," her mother suddenly suggested from the kitchen doorway.

"What I'm going to do is muzzle him," Mara quipped while rinsing her hands under the spigot.

Behind her, she heard Nick's introduction. "This is my sister."

Mara didn't try to muster up a smile before pivoting to meet her brother's great find.

"Mara." Nick beamed. "This is Eric Lassiter."

Her heart quickened as her gaze longingly swept over Rick. He looked different. While there was a tranquility in his expression, she was caught up in turmoil.

"Guess I'll leave you two alone," Nick murmured and backed up.

Rick searched her eyes for a hint of the warmth usually in them. "I know what you said before, but I had to come back."

She wavered, uncertain even as she ached for him to open his arms to her. "Where were you?"

"Miami." As she stared at him, a flicker of uncertainty in her eyes, he told himself he was making progress. She hadn't fled at the sight of him this time. "I had a few things to settle there. Now, I'm back."

"I read the newspaper story. You were in danger."

"With me, you could have been, too. But I'm through with all that. No more running around the country. I was ready to tell Carl that I was through running. I had enough of it, and if they couldn't protect me, then that was the end of it, but that end was better than giving up forever everything that I'd found here, better than living without you, without Jessie."

She thought about the loving way he'd watched and held Jessie, as if she were his own.

Unable to stand the silence hanging in the air, he bent over the playpen to Jessie. "Hi, sweetheart." Lightly he stroked her forehead. "That would have been a crummy life for her."

Kicking her legs, Jessie cooed and smiled back at him.

"Looks like one Vincotti still likes me," he said with a lightness he didn't feel. Straightening, he met Mara's stare again. "I can start a new life." Rick ventured closer and raised his hands out to her in an appealing gesture. "I couldn't ask you to give up everything—friends and family—for me. I couldn't ask you and Jessie to run with me."

Mara uttered the thought haunting her. "I don't really know you, do I?"

"You know me," he said firmly. "Does it matter that I do something else for a living or that my name isn't what you thought it was? I'm the same man who held you and loved you." He drew a long breath. "I wanted to tell you about everything. I planned to, but Carl came in and—'' He couldn't believe how badly he was fumbling around for words. He'd made a living for years with nothing more than words. "You gave more than I ever expected, and I could offer you nothing," he said, trying to explain. He was dying to touch her. Even the strands of her hair tempted him, but he didn't move closer, not yet.

As he captured her eyes with his steadfast stare, Mara longed to feel his arms around her. "You were the one who was always helping me."

With a shake of his head, Rick released a quick, short laugh. "No, Mara. You helped me. You put a reason for everything that had happened to me back into my life. I was existing until I met you." He grimaced and forced to the surface what still gnawed at him. "And I hurt you. I hurt you in a way that's almost unforgivable. But I'm asking you to forgive me. Hell, I'll beg, if that's what it takes."

So much had happened since she'd last seen him. She'd learned so much about him, and about herself. She knew now that the doubts hadn't been meant for him but for herself. Because of Steve, she'd stopped trusting her own judgment. She understood now why she'd given him no chance to explain. She'd been too afraid to rely on her ability to discern truth from lies. So she'd assumed everything he would tell her would be a lie. "It's not often someone meets a person who believes in truth at any price, even his safety, his life."

She took the first step, closing the distance between them until only inches separated them. With a hesitant touch, she set her hand on his chest. "I've missed you. I didn't want to, because I couldn't believe you would hurt me that way. But I did miss you. And I do love you.''

Those were the words he'd been waiting for. Tugging her to him, he promised, ''No more secrets.''

She wavered between joy and uncertainty. ''What happens now?''

He laughed softly against her cheek. ''This happens now,'' he murmured and closed his mouth over hers. He kissed her gently even as he hungered. ''I have a new job, here, at a local newspaper. Now I have only one problem.'' Tenderly he pressed his lips to the faint line creasing her forehead. ''Would you be willing to change your name?''

On a laugh, Mara tossed back her head and caressed the nape of his neck. ''Eric Lassiter,'' she said, trying out the name. ''I like it.''

With her touch, pleasure swept through him. ''How much? Will you and Jessie make a life with me?''

Mara clung to him. ''There's no one else we would rather be with forever,'' she assured him. Her heart pounding with happiness, she coiled her arms around his neck and drew him close for another kiss. This one was wild, demanding more than just the fleeting bliss of passion. Mara felt the promise of forever in his kiss and mentally laughed with a private thought. Her family had been right. There was a special man not only for her but also for Jessie—a very special and loving man.

* * * * *

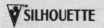

SILHOUETTE

SPECIAL EDITION ®

COMING NEXT MONTH

EXPECTANT FATHER Leanne Banks

In one shocking night, Glory Danson and Caleb Masters made a baby!
Caleb was a brilliant scientist bent on saving the world—certainly not
father material. Could a tiny infant turn this confirmed bachelor into a
family man?

SUMMERS PAST Laurey Bright

When Seth Keegan returned home after years in prison, he expected his
mother's scorn and the neighbours' glares. But he was shocked to find
Ghislaine Pargiter, the woman he'd once loved, living high in his
family house, her young daughter mysteriously the heir to the Keegan
fortune...

NEW BRIDE IN TOWN Amy Frazier

Sweet Hope Weddings

Belle Sherman decided to live life to the full and moved to Sweet Hope
to do just that. This recently jilted bride had almost given up hope of
finding—and keeping—Mr Right. But when she met sexy Boone
O'Malley, Belle knew this was one eligible bachelor she couldn't let
pass her by!

MARRY ME, NOW! Allison Hayes

Nick Reynolds was Dacy Fallon's first love, the man she could never
forget. They'd been just seventeen when life had taken them on
different paths. Now fate had brought Dacy back to town—and she was
determined to reclaim her man...

MOLLY DARLING Laurie Paige

That's My Baby!

When scandal threatened Sam Frazier's custody of his child, a marriage
of convenience to Molly Clelland made her an instant, loving mum.
But would sexy Sam ever make the strait-laced schoolteacher his
blushing, breathless bride?

RAINSINGER Ruth Wind

Winona Snow came to New Mexico expecting to claim her inheritance
and establish a new life for herself and her troubled young sister. Love
was the last thing she wanted. But she hadn't bargained on Daniel
Lynch, the new resident in her abandoned house...

GET 4 BOOKS AND A SILVER PLATED PHOTO FRAME

Return this coupon and we'll send you 4 Silhouette Special Edition® novels and a silver plated photo frame absolutely FREE! We'll even pay the postage and packing for you.

We're making you this offer to introduce you to the benefits of Reader Service: FREE home delivery of brand-new Silhouette® romances, at least a month before they are available in the shops, FREE gifts and a monthly Newsletter packed with information.

Accepting these FREE books and gift places you under no obligation to buy, you may cancel at any time, even after receiving just your free shipment. Simply complete the coupon below and send it to:

SILHOUETTE READER SERVICE, FREEPOST, CROYDON, SURREY, CR9 3WZ.

No stamp needed

Yes, please send me 4 free Silhouette Special Edition novels and a silver plated photo frame. I understand that unless you hear from me, I will receive 6 superb new titles every month for just £2.30* each postage and packing free. I am under no obligation to purchase any books and I may cancel or suspend my subscription at any time, but the free books and gifts will be mine to keep in any case. (I am over 18 years of age)

E61E

Ms/Mrs/Miss/Mr _____

Address _____

_____

_____ Postcode _____

mps MAILING PREFERENCE SERVICE

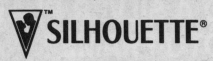